CHANGES

CHANGES

K.L. Burt

To order additional copies of this book, contact:
Xlibris
1-888-795-4274
www.Xlibris.com
Orders@Xlibris.com
540404

Contents

CHAPTER 1

Damn

"Damn! How I'ma get out of this shit? Didn't seem this hard in the beginning. Oh well, fuck it. Nothing to it but to do it as they say."

"Man, shut the fuck up and pass me the sticks. It's my turn, nigga."

"Nigga, it's your turn when I say it's your turn. I'm just trying to get used to this fat-ass joystick nigga. I'm used to the PlayStation sticks—a lot more compact."

"Ain't gonna matter. Still gonna bust ya ass."

"Whatever, nigga. I'm tired of playing anyway."

"Then give me the sticks then."

"Here, nigga."

"Anyway, nigga, you been thinking about what we discussed last week?"

"Yeah, man, been thinking a lot about it. Shit is getting real rough around here, and a nigga like me needs that cream."

"Yo, K-Block, we can do this, man. Can't none of these little niggas around here fuck with us, man. We can put this whole thing on smash. I gots the connections, you gots the plans, and we both gots the muscle. We can have the whole Philly drug game on smash, man."

"Yeah, I know. I see these nut-ass niggas running this shit getting paid and dumb as shit. I know we could get a lock on this thing inside a four or five months. But this ain't the the time, D."

"Shit, Block, then when is the time? A nigga is hungry right now, but I ain't making no moves without you."

"Yeah, nigga, I know. And I'm starving out here too, but now ain't the time. Tryin' to make the right moves for once in my life. Your sister, the kids.

I can't risk getting popped on some bullshit-ass charges, and as tempting as it is, I can't get into this shit and risk losing what's most important to me. The whole reason I would do it anyway is for the fam. Can't lose them not over no dumb shit."

"You right, nigga, but think about it anyway. We are way smarter than the niggas that is running things now. I'm just saying we could do this shit, man. It's in me. It's in my blood, nigga."

"Yeah, I know but you can't always listen to blood. You don't wanna be like your brother, Rock, in and out of jail, homeless, beating up on his baby's momma all the time. He ain't got a pot to piss in nor a window to throw it out of, D. Can't follow your blood all the time."

"Yeah, I know, but I know we could make this thing work."

"All right, nigga, I be out. Your sister's cooking dinner, and I'm hungry as shit."

"All right, nigga, get at me tomorrow."

"Later."

"Peace."

The man K-Block, a.k.a. Block, his government name Kelly Treshawn Brown. Who could know that this man was the product of a God-fearing family, a son of a Baptist pastor father and a choir director mother and a successful sister attorney, a husband to a good woman, and a father of two precious children. Who would have guessed that in a matter of three short years from this very conversation he had with his brother-in-law, D (government name Devon Lewis Karr), that he would be the biggest, most violent drug lord that the streets of Philadelphia would ever know. After all, how do you go from a mild-mannered father of two to a sadistic killer? Well, it doesn't happen overnight, and it damn sure doesn't happen all at once. It's like that Chinese water torture—it happens on drop at a time.

Ring, ring!
"Yeah, what's up, babe?"
"You leave D's house yet?"
"Yeah, babe."
"You coming straight home?"
"Yeah, babe."
"Could you stop and get some bread?"
"Yeah, babe. Anything else?"
"No, baby, just the bread, and hurry home."
"Okay, babe, see you soon."

"Damn, I'm hungry as shit. She knows I hate stopping at the store for shit when I'm hungry. Oh well, guess I should stop bitchin' about it and just hurry up. Damn, I'm starving."

"Hey, baby, I missed you. Did you bring the bread?"

"Yeah, babe, I got the bread. Now give me some sugar."

"Eeeeeel!" squeals Kelly Jr. and his twin sister, Kayla.

"Eeeeel what?"

"Eeeeel, y'all kissing! That's nasty."

"Y'all should be glad we kissing. That's how you got here," says Shandra. "That's right! In fact, give me a little more of that sugar."

Damn! Shan sure had talent with that tongue among other things, but she could always make my dick hard with just a kiss.

"Eeeeel!" the kids screamed again as Kelly now chased them around the house.

"Okay, children, you too Kelly, go wash your hands and get ready to eat."

"Okay, Mom," the kids said in unison.

"Okay, Mom." Kelly mimicked the kids. She smiled. "Damn! How I miss that."

"After dinner, me and Twist are going to the bar."

And there goes my good mood. "The bar again? You know I don't like you hanging out in bars and clubs, especially with that damn Twist. And what the fuck kind of name is that for a grown woman? The bitch is four hundred pounds, with seven kids with six different baby daddies. This is some bullshit!"

"Why do we always have to fight when I want to go out? Not everybody is a homebody like you, and after being around kids all day, I needs to get out and have some adult conversation."

"Adult conversation? So I'm not adult enough for you to conversate with like your loose-ass, big-ass sister and all those motherfuckers at the bar."

"Babe, you know you likes to be left alone when you have off. And talking to you is like talking to a wall sometimes. I tried to include you, but you don't like hanging out, so what do you want me to do?"

"I just don't believe a married woman should be hanging out in clubs and bars. Certain things you leave behind when you're married. You can't, or I should say, shouldn't do the same things you did when you were single."

"Well, I'm sorry I don't feel the same way. I'll be back by two."

This is some ol' bullshit leaving me home to babysit while she hits the club. I left all that bullshit behind with I got married—the clubs, the strip joints, the

whoring, the tricking, etc., and she can't even stay out of a bar. This is some ol'
bullshit.

A few hours later....

Damn! It's five o'clock already gotta get up. Look at her sleeping like a baby.
She should be coming in here at three o'clock a.m. How did I know? 'cause I was
awake, pretending like I wasn't up all night waiting for her to get home safe. And
she comes slithering into bed horny, wanting some dick before going to sleep. I
started not to give her none, but of course, I did as usual. Fuck going to pay for all
that early-morning fucking. Tired as shit and got ten hours to go.

Shit! Job is good. Just doesn't motivate me to get it going this early in the
morning. Oh well, gotta get going anyway. Kids gotta eat. Hope the car starts this
morning. Don't feel like catching the bus. Cold as shit out here. Come on, come on,
start! Yes! This might be a good day after all.

Damn! I love that man. Every day he gets up, goes to work, takes care of my
kids, sexes me up how I like. But . . . how come I fell so alone? Even when he is
here, he is somewhere else. Maybe he regrets . . . ? No, no, no. Can't start thinking
like that. He is a good man, and I know he really, truly loves me and my kids
but . . . Can't stop now. Gotta get these kids up and ready for school, then off to
another day at this bullshit job. I love my man, but damn, I really wish he made
more money—a lot more like them ballers at the bar and the club. Damn! Them
Jamaican and Trini dudes work like six to seven jobs and send the money back
home to support their family. Even if they do keep one or two side chicks around,
family comes first to them. Real good providers. Damn, even their jump-off's be
gettin that cheese from them. Real, real good providers. Anyway that's them.
Besides I'm done with those niggas anyway, even if I do party with them once and
a while. They are the best dudes to party with. If Kelly only knew. He gets upset
with the little one or two times a week I go out. If he only knew back in the day it
was Sunday to Sunday with me. Partying like no tomorrow. Drinking like a fish,
just me and Twist fucking and sucking all them ballers and Jamaicans. Damn, that
was some good dick back then. If he only knew I used to get drunk as shit and fuck
like six big-dicked dudes a night. I was a bad bitch back then—two or three of them
thick-dicked motherfuckers at a time. Whoooa! Anyway, that was then and this is
now. Oh shit! My pussy wet.

"Yoooo, D! What's crackin, bro?" hollered Rock as he approached.
"Ain't nothing, Rock. What's good with you?" D replied.
"Ain't nothing. Just trying to get this paper out here. Tricking these
bitches, you know."

"Yeah, I know. How's the kids?" inquired D.

"They all right. Baby mom's trippin' again. Had to bust her ass just this morning for talking shit. Gonna question me about where I was last night and talking that shit like I should have stayed with that bitch and how she gonna put me out a shit. Yo, that bitch crazy. I bust her right in her fuckin' mouth," said Rock.

"Yo, Rock, you crazy, man. What you keep fucking that bitch up for? You gonna fuck around and be right back in jail over that shit," said D.

"Yo, man, you know I don't give a fuck about that jail shit. The county like a summer home and upstate like a winter one. I fuck niggas up in there just like on these streets. Niggas know not to fuck with Rock. I crack a nigga's head wide open on these streets and bust a nigga's ass in the joint then fuck the shit out of them an' make them punk asses give me head with the shit still on my dick!" Rock exclaimed.

"Damn! Rock, the joint done turned you out into a straight fag," said D.

"Man, fuck you, nigga! I ain't no faggot!" yelled Rock.

"Naw, nigga, you ain't fucking me. And if you ain't no faggot, then what do you call it then?" said D.

"Man, fuck you, nigga! I ain't no fag, and if you say that shit again, I'ma beat your ass."

"Fuck you, Rock, I ain't one of them bitch-ass niggas that hang around you. Scared you gonna snap as usual and fuck one of them up. You know I rumble like you rumble, nigga. You know it's whatever with me," said D.

"Yo, you one crazy young bull, D! You lucky I love ya and you my brother, or it would be some shit right now."

"Yeah, I know. Whatever, nigga."

"All right, nigga. Be easy. I'll holla at ya later."

"All right, Rock. Later."

Damn! That nigga Rock is throwed the fuck off. K-Block is right. I don't wanna follow in that nigga's footsteps, no way, no how. But I still wanna get this paper out here though. Damn. Wish Block was down with this shit. We'd be fuckin' millionaires out this bitch. Damn!

On the other side of town, Kelly sat in his car with a cardboard box of this-and-that from a cleaned-out desk sitting on the front seat next to him and thought, *Damn! Laid off. What the fuck is this shit? Okay, Kelly, don't panic. Hold it together. It's cool. Just cause the CEO of the company says no more layoffs after the last bunch of layoffs don't mean shit. Just because I'm in debt up to my eyeballs don't mean nothing. Just 'cause the fams need the benefits. It's cool . . . Fuck, shit, fucking motherfuckers! Damn! What the fuck am I supposed to do? Hold up,*

Kelly. Keep it together. Remember, you ain't no slouch. You have marketable skills. You'll bounce right back from this. Shit, maybe some time off is just what you need. Yeah, that's it. That's what I'll do. Take a little time off, enjoy myself. I can apply for unemployment the first thing in the morning, and it should be more than enough to maintain us for a couple of weeks. Yeah, that's it. I'll take about a week off and chill and pound the pavement next week, and I'll have a new J-O-B in no time. This layoff might actually be a blessing in disguise.

CHAPTER 2

365

"Kelly, Kelly, *Kelly*, wake up!"

"Yeah, what? Hey, babe, what you doing home so early?"

"Early? Kelly, it's after four o'clock p.m. I'm coming home from work. Have you been asleep all day?" said an obviously upset Shan.

"Naw, babe, of course not. I had gotten up right after you this morning, all set to pound the pavement, but I started to feel a little sick, so I lay back down," explained Kelly. "Before I knew it, it was two o'clock p.m. I got up, got the kids from school, and lay back down. No sense trying to go job hunting today. Just got too late on me. I'll definitely go tomorrow. Anyway, how was your day?"

"Same as usual, shitty! I go back and forth every day to a job I hate making scraps and . . ."

"And what, babe?" asked Kelly.

"Nothing!" exclaimed Shan.

"No, it was definitely something, so tell me."

"Nothing, babe, just drop it. I'ma take a shower and get dinner ready. You know, since you home now, it would be nice if you made dinner for me every once in a while," said Shan.

"You're absolutely right, babe. I'll start doing that, but don't get used to it. Once I start working again, it will be business as usual," said Kelly.

Ring!

"Hello," answered Kelly.

"Yo, Block, you coming through today or what?" said D on the other end.

"Yeah, nigga. Had to wait for wifey to get home. You know I can't leave the kids," said Kelly.

"Yeah, I know, nigga. Just hurry up and get here. Shit, I'm bored as hell."

"So, nigga, I'm not the fuck here to entertain you just wait," said Kelly.

"Yo, nigga, don't leave me hangin."

"Okay, nigga, got damn you sound like my bitch or something."

"Fuck you, nigga!" exclaimed D. "An' just get here, okay?"

"All right, nigga, I'm on my way," replied Kelly.

Click.

"Yo, babe, save me a plate. I'm heading out."

"Where you going? To D's house again?" questioned Shan.

"Yeah. What's the problem?"

"The problem is you spend more time with my brother than with me and the kids, not to mention . . . You know what? Just go on. Whatever, just go on."

"Be back later," said Kelly.

Shit. What is her problem now? If it ain't one thing, it's another with her. I just know she ain't tripping about me still being unemployed. Ain't my fault the job market is slow right now. What the hell she tripping for anyway? My unemployment still going strong. Money still coming in. That bitch crazy.

"Twist, I had to tell you this ol' fly shit. I come home and again—"

"What? That nigga still ain't got off his ass to look for a job?" asked Twist.

"Yeah, telling me he got up this morning feeling sick so he laid back down. Yo, that lazy motherfucker is trippin'. How stupid does he think I am? Oh! And peep this. He was so sick, he slept till the kids got out of school and then again till I got home, and now that nigga's over D's house again."

"No, the fuck he didn't," said Twist.

"Yes, the fuck he did, girl. I work all day and come home to this lazy-ass nigga in the bed. Muthafucka couldn't even make dinner."

"Yo, girl, I told you that's why you need a nigga on the side. You know me. I keeps two or four niggas at all times 'cause if one starts acting up, I just move on to the next one. And you know them island niggas keeps a girl looking fresh. Shit, give them niggas some pussy and a little head and consider yourself a kept woman, ya know," said Twist.

"Yeah, girl, I know," replied Shan. "That's why I started fucking with that Jamaican nigga at the bar. That nigga been trying to fuck me for years, talking all that good shit of how he will pay my bills and get my hair and nails done and shit. Even said he'll take care of my kids and shit. What's a bitch to do? Besides, the only things Kelly had going for him was a good job with benefits and his dick game was the bomb. But he ain't had a job nor made me cum in 365."

"Shit, girl, if even his dick game done got weak, then why you staying around?" asked Twist.

"Shit, my kids seem to like the nigga, and I don't want to go nowhere till I'm sure this Jamaican isn't just talking shit. Sure I gave him a little pussy and let him eat it and got a little cash out his ass, but moving in is another thing. Besides not many niggas would take care of another man's kids. Even though he is talking a good game, I can't trust it just yet. Shit, the only reason Kelly takes care of these little muthafuckas is because he don't know they ain't his." Shan said.

"Yo, D, 'sup nigga?"

"Chillin', chillin'. What's good wit' you, Block?"

"Ain't nothing, man. Just same ol' bullshit at the crib. Your sister is a trip, my nigga."

"Yo, you ain't gotta tell me. I know," said D.

"Yeah, man. She just be on some ol' bullshit since I been laid off, always coming at me 'bout getting a job and shit. She act like I don't have no money coming in at all. Mad 'cause she gotta go to her bullshit job every day and still gets paid less than I do collecting unemployment. Talking all that shit every day, stepping on my nuts, ya know?"

"Yeah, man, I dig. Keep ya head up though. Don't let it stress ya."

"Oh, don't worry about that shit, it won't. That bitch don't know how good she got it with me. Ain't no other nigga gonna put up with her shit like I do."

"I dig, bro. Yo, man, fuck all that shit. Let's have a brew."

"Now that's the best thing I heard all day."

Seven hours and several six-packs later . . .

"Yo, Block, all I'm sayin is—yo, all I'm sayin is, now is the time we can do this shit, man. I mean what the *fuck*. What you got to lose, nigga? You ain't got no job. Now is the perfect fuckin' time."

"Naw, nigga, still don't feel right. I'll let you know when it's time. In fact, niiggggaaa, you will be the first to know. So stop stressing me, man," said Kelly.

"Yo, all I'm saying is—" said D as Kelly cut him off.

"Yeah, nigga, I know what you saying. What, you think I don't want this paper too? Shit, nigga, it's fucking crunch time. I needs this paper now more than ever. I just think we can get at it another way, without all the drama that taking over these streets is gonna bring. You know I'ma definitely get it together and get it, and you know that if I eats, you eats," said Kelly.

"Yeah, I know, nigga, but I'm hungry right now, man. These niggas out here ain't got nothing for us, man, ya know?" said D.

"I know, man, and you know, even if we did decide to do this thing today or tomorrow, it's gonna take some preparation, making sure that all the i's are dotted and all the t's are crossed, ya know? I ain't doing no time on no ol' bullshit like these little niggas out here be doing, ya heard?" said Kelly

"Yeah, man, I hear you on that. But fuck that, man! We would have shit so tight, man, we would never go down, ya know?" said D.

"Yeah, nigga, it would have to be that tight for me to get involved in it, but I ain't no fool. Never say never."

"Yo, guess I better head back to the crib. Wifey probably pissed at me. Still gonna try and get me some and take my ass back to sleep. I'll holla at you later," said Kelly as he got up, heading for the door.

"All right, Block. Be easy, man, and keep thinking about what I said. Man, we could be *kings* out here," said D.

"All right, nigga, peace," said Kelly.

"Peace!"

"*Shit*, you going out again!" said an obviously pissed and drunk Kelly.

"And why wouldn't I?" said Shan. "Didn't you just come in from drinking wit' D? Shit, I've been working all day. I deserve some time to relax too. Kids are asleep. Be back at the usual time." *Slam!*

Shit! Guess I won't be getting no pussy tonight. Shit, my dick hard as a muthafucka too. Shit, can't go to sleep like this. Time to reach for the 'stash o' dirt.' Just what a nigga need during these trying times. Let me see. What will it be tonight? Big ASS Bitches 3 or Brazilian Street Whores 7? Maybe a little of both.

Meanwhile, Shan stormed out the house, walking quickly down the street and around the corner so as not to be seen by anybody who might be looking.

"Sup, babe,!" said a dark-skinned man.

"Sup!" answered Shan.

"How you been?"

"Fine! I missed you," said Shan flirtatiously.

"Missed you too, babe. I mean, I really missed you," said the dark-skinned man.

"I know what you mean. So no bar tonight, huh?"

"No, luv, straight to da house. Got something long and hard to give you."

"Good, 'cause I got something wet and deep to give to you."

"Sounds real good to me, girl. How about sucking on some of dis big dick while I drive."

"Again? Remember, the last time you almost crashed and killed us both. You came so hard."

"I know, baby, but I won do dat again."

"You promise!"

"Yeah, baby, I promise."

"Well, okay." *Zzziiipp.* "Oh my, you really did miss me. *Mmmmmmmmmmm!*" *Slurp, slurp, slurp.* "*Mmmmmmmmmm.*"

"Whooooh, shit! You missed me too I see, baby. Oh yeah, oh yeah."

"Oh yeah! Oh shit, here it comes! Whoooh, damn! Nothing like my fuckin porn. But it will never take the place of that good ol' pussy. But I guess it will have to do for now. Shit, Shandra better start acting right, or I'ma have to get me a jump-off or something. Beating my meat just don't cut it all the time."

"Oh yeah! Oh yeah! Oh *shit!* Damn, baby, your dick is so big, your dick is sooooo biiiiigggggg! Fuck me! Ohhhh! Fuck me hardddd! Yeah, daddy, oh shit!"

"Yeah, baby, you love dis big dick in that pussy?"

"Yessss, daddy! Oh! Yeeeeeessssssss!"

"You my bitch?" questioned the dark-skinned man.

"Yeah, daddy, I'm your fucking bitch, I'm your fucking whore. Fuck me, daddy, harder, harder! Owwww, yeah. Stick that big-ass dick in my ass, daddy. Yesssssss. Oh shit, daddy, I'm cumming again. Oh shit, this dick is sooooo goooood. Yeah, daddy, you about to cum? Put it in my mouth. Put it in my mouth!"

"*Ohhhhh shhhhhhiiiiiittttttt!*"

"Yes, big daddy! You fuck me so fucking good."

"Yeah, baby, you ain't never had it like dis, have you?" asked the dark-skinned man.

"No, daddy, never!" exclaimed Shan.

"Shit, you know you love this shit."

"Yeah, daddy, I love it. Fuck you make me cum so fuckin' hard, daddy."

"I know, baby. You suck dis dick real, good make me cum like volcano. So when you gonna stop all da playing around wit' me and leave that lame-ass boy and come live wit' me?"

"You really want me here like that?" questioned Shan. "You know I got kids and shit and fuck all that. The sex is great, but I can't leave my kids behind."

"No problem, baby. Your kids are more than welcome too," said the dark-skinned man.

"You mean that shit?"

"You know I do."

"Don't just be saying that 'cause I take it real serious when it comes to my kids," said Shan, sitting up in the bed and looking intently into his eyes.

"Look, girl, you know I love you, and fucking you is the best, so just stop playing fucking games and move in wit' me," said the dark skinned man, sitting up and looking her back in the eyes.

"I really want to, but I have to give it some thought," said Shan, looking away.

"Don't think too long, girl. I need you wit' me. And I'm getting tired of fucking da shit out of you and sending you home to dat lame ass. I would rather fuck the shit out of you, rest, and fuck some more like we about to do now."

"Oh really!"

"Yes, really. Don't play. Open dem fucking legs and let me suck that wet-ass pussy dry"

"Ohhhhhhhhh shhhhitttt!"

CHAPTER 3

What the Fuck?

Yawn! "Shit, what time is it? Shandra? Shan?" *What the fuck?* exclaimed Kelly as he rolled over to Shandra's side of the bed to look at the clock. *It's fucking four o'clock in the morning an' that bitch ain't got home yet? This is some ol' bullshit! I'ma straight cuss that bitch the fuck out when she get here. What the fuck kind of bullshit is this? She know I don't play these fucking games shit. Butttt what if something happened to her? Damn. She know I hate her going out all late and shit. Twist stay with that drama going on! What if something happened to my baby? Shit, I'll give it a few more minutes than I'ma have to start calling around and shit.* Click goes the sound of the lock on the door being opened, interrupting Kelly's thought.

"Hey, baby, what you doing up?"

"What am I doing up? Do you know what fucking time it is?"

"Yeah, baby, I know, and I'm sorry I'm late. Me and Twist went to this new club she heard about in Jersey, and you know, we got lost on the way home."

"Yeah!"

"Yeah, babe, we was all turned around and shit. I just wanted to get home to my baby and my bed. I'm so fucking tired."

"Okay, as long as you all right!" said Kelly, feeling guilty about his earlier thoughts.

"I'm fine, baby. Don't worry about me."

"I have to worry, babe. Can't have nothing happen to you," said Kelly, feeling whipped.

"Ohhhhh! You so sweet! Go on to sleep, baby. I'm fine. I'm gonna get a shower, then I'ma join you."

"All right, babe. Good night."

"Good night, baby," said Shan, slipping quickly out of her clothes and into the shower.

Whew! Glad that nigga ain't wanna fuck tonight. I didn't have a chance to shower fucking with that nigga. Would have had to fuck again without it. That was close. Don't like doing that shit too much. It'll get me busted sooner or later. Gotta douche the shit out of my pussy tonight. That muthafucka came a got damn river inside of me. Shit better not get me pregnant again. Them abortions hard to cover up, thought Shan, and she reached for the Summer's Eve.

Shit, I'm so tired. Something about that fucking woman. She can play the shit out of me if she wants, and I will fall for it every time. Most niggas would be mad as shit they bitch come in off the streets at some four o'clock in the morning. Got myself all ready to cuss that bitch out. Then here my punk ass go, worrying about the bitch's well-being. Then, of course, she has the perfect explanation. Shit. Fuck it now too tired to argue anyway, Kelly thought as he fell back to sleep.

A few blocks away, at D's house . . .

Bang, bang, bang, bang, bang, bang!

"Yo, D!"

Bang, bang, bang!

"Yo, D! Open the fuckin' door, nigga."

Bang, bang, bang!

"Yo, what the fuck? Who the fuck banging on my got damn door like that?" D yelled as he hung his head out his bedroom window.

"Yo, D! It's Rock."

"Yo, Rock, nigga, what the fuck is your problem bangin' on my fucking door like that fucking five o'clock in the morning. Nigga, is you crazy?"

"Yo, D, let me in, man. Shit is real hectic."

"Yo, nigga, you know my lady don't even like you and damn sure don't want you in her house this early in the morning."

"Yo, D, fuck that bitch, nigga. I'm your blood. Open the fuckin' door."

"Yo, nigga, I don't give a fuck who you are. Don't talk that shit about my lady."

"All right, nigga, all right. Just open the fuckin' door. Damn."

"Hold up. I be right down."

Click! "Damn, nigga! Shit, I'd been dead already if niggas was on my ass like that." Says Rock, as he pushes inside the house and closes the door.

"Yo, nigga, what's the fucking emergency that it couldn't wait till later?"

"Yo, D! I gotta lay low here for a couple of days, yo. These niggas from North think I fucked up this money for these grams I sold. Fact is, my bitch got at the cash and spent it. Shit, you know me. I'm like, fuck a supplier, nigga. I bust this nigga's ass in a rumble, but this nigga done called a damn army on me. Muthafuckas done ran up in my baby's mom's crib and shit wit them thangs, so you know, I threw some shells at them niggas. Dropped one or two of 'em, then I broke out."

"You broke out? What about your kids and Nessa?"

"My kids is with they granmoms. Nessa is with her sister. I was in the crib all by myself when this shit went down. Shit, nigga, you know I wouldn't be here if my kids was there. Yo, I gotta use your phone to make sure Nessa don't go home for a couple of days."

"Shit, nigga, go ahead, but I don't know about you staying here and shit. You know my girl don't like your ass."

"Yeah, nigga, I know, but try and look out for me, nigga. I am your only brother after all."

You most definitely my brother. But not my only one, D thought. *Damn. What the fuck I'ma do with this nigga? Can't leave him out in the cold. He is my brother after all. Shit. Guess I better go get this over wit'. Gonna have to fuck the shit out of her tonight to get her to agree to this shit.*

Later that evening…

"What the fuck? Nottaaa, nigga. Ain't no fucking way that nigga staying the fuck up in here. No fuckin' way. I don't give a shit whose brother he is. Got my kids all up in here, and bullshit stay following that fuckin' nigga. No, D. No fuckin' way."

"Look, babe, this your house and all according to the papers and shit, but I pay the fuckin' bills an' I ain't leavin' my brother hangin' like that. Now it's only for a couple of days. You two can bear each other that long, I know."

"No, D."

"'No, D?' What the fuck, you thought I was askin'? Naw, bitch, you got it twisted. I was informing you of what's goin' down. Like it or not, Rock gonna be here for a couple of days. Case closed."

"But, D!"

"No fuckin' *but*s. Now I told you how it's goin' down. Deal with it."

"But I don't wanna deal with it," she said, pouting.

"Come here, girl. You heard what I said." Then D proceeded to do just what he knew he would have to do to close the deal with her.

D's girl Tracy was one bad bitch, and not just because of her double-D tits and triple-fat ass, but the bitch was fucking beautiful. She could easily be America's next top model, hands down. D never wondered how he pulled such a bad bitch, being broke and shit. His game was airtight, and he didn't look too bad his damn self. He was used to pulling fine-looking girls all the time, but Tracy was extra fine. But other than his game, D was smart, real smart, when it came to women, and he knew how to get in good with the ones he wanted.

Tracy, as fine as she was, had really low self-esteem that came from her kids' father, who didn't do nothing but cheat on her and beat her ass when he wanted to. That on top of the mental abuse, he let her know as often as he could that won't no man want no bitch with four kids that ain't theirs. She stayed with that nigga till her oldest was ten. Tracy wasn't but twenty-three herself. An' when D met her, he keyed right in on her self-esteem issues and proceeded to make her feel like the smartest, most beautiful, most wanted woman on the planet. And after that, he had her hooked.

D did his dirt, of course, but he always came home to wifey. After all, when he met her, he didn't have a pot to piss in or a window to throw that shit out of, and she fell for him so hard and fast, she moved him right in with her and her four kids in a house her parents left her before they died.

"Come here, girl. Get some of this good ol' hard candy that I got for ya." D was a freak, and he ate a lot of pussy in his time, but for some reason, he wouldn't eat out Tracy. It was all good to her though, 'cause it gave her more time in their foreplay to do what she loved to do, and that was sucking dick like a fuckin' Hoover. She grabbed at D's thick long hard shaft quick and fast and got right to work on it.

First playing with the head with her tongue, lickin' up and down and all around before taking all his hardness inside her mouth, sucking and slurping like a madwoman. Tracy was no doubt a pro at sucking dick, but D would never give her the satisfaction of cummin' in her mouth, not because he didn't want to, but he wanted to always leave just a little bit of doubt in her mind as to whether she was pleasing him or not. Please believe, with the way Tracy sucked dick, it would make the strongest man nut a river, but D held out, making her work all the harder to please her man.

After she got his dick good and stiff, D flipped her on her stomach and slowly slid his big dick up and down her swollen, wet pussy. By the way that clit was throbbing, he knew she was about to cum. No longer wanting to tease, he slid his stiff member into her waiting pussy, and almost on cue, she came so fuckin' hard, he thought she had peed on him. But still wanting to please her man, she begged for more. Pounding harder and harder in and out, the juices from Tracy's now drenched canal was spurting all over, but that didn't stop the show as D continued his onslaught of that pussy that he knew was his. Tracy's loud moans of pleasure just turned him on more. Now with her pussy sufficiently pounded and open, he moved on to a tighter hole. Sliding his wet, long shaft from her gaping virgina, he slid it upward to her asshole and stuffed the whole thing in. Tracy screamed with delight and came again and again. Pounding over and over, each stroke more merciless than that last until he finally let out a loud, thunderous roar and let his lady know he just bust. As if she needed any more signs, the hot injection of cum in her ass let her know all she needed to know: that this was her dick.

Chapter 4

I Need Dat

"Yo, K-Block! 'Sup, my nigga!"

"Chillin', Chillin'."

"Yo, dog, got Rock stayin' at the spot for a minute. Been like a whole week now."

"What the fuck for?"

"Yo, dog, this nigga done got into some shit out here in these streets an'—"

"An' let me guess, that nigga needs a place to hide out for a while," interjected Kelly.

"Yeah. Well, you know, he's my bro. Can't leave him hangin'," said D.

"I feel you, dog. Just make sure that nigga don't leave you hangin'."

"I dig. Anyway, where you been? Ain't seen you in a min."

"Just been chillin', you know, looking for another job. Shandra been on my shit lately, pissin' me off an' shit about this job thing. I ain't had no pussy in like a month," said Kelly, obvious frustration in his tone.

"A month? Damn, nigga, you got a jump-off or something?"

"Nigga, I wish! I been beatin' my dick like crazy. She been going out more and more and stayin' out later and later, and everytime I step to her about it, she gots some damn excuse to explain it all away. But on the real, I think she fuckin' around on me."

"Get the fuck out of here, nigga! No fuckin' way! Me and my sis ain't always seen eye to eye, but I know she loves you and wouldn't do no shit like that to you."

"I don't know man. I know as horny as I am she gots to be hornier than a muthafucker but she ain't been givin' none to me. So all I can think is she givin' it to someone else."

"Naw, nigga, that ain't it. I know. You talked to her about this shit?"

"Naw, I don't wanna start accusing her of shit when I ain't got no proof, but shit just ain't right between us, and I'm starting to feel like she playin' me."

"Naw, nigga, you wrong," said D. "I ain't belivin' that shit. Y'all been together too long. Shit, y'all practically raised my crazy ass, and I know she loves you too much for that bullshit, my nigga. You know I don't vouch for no one especially no bitch, but I vouch for her, yameen."

"I feel ya, nigga. I hope you right though, 'cause if you ain't, it's gonna be hell to pay."

"Nigga, if she cheatin' on you, I'll fuckin' load ya gunz the fuck up for ya!"

"Word!" exclaimed Kelly.

"Word!" responded D.

"Twist!"

"Sup! I think I'm about to leave Kelly!"

"Whaaaaat! Are you for real?"

"Yeah, I think so!"

"What do you mean you think so? Either you are or you aren't—there is no 'I think about it.'"

"Yo, Twist, Raz been talking that good shit and showin' me mad love. Buying me and my kids shit. Can't take any of that shit home though. An' me an' Kelly ain't fucked in over a month and Raz been putting it on me, girl, butttt . . ."

"But what?"

"I still love Kelly."

"Girl, forget that love shit. If a nigga is willin' to pay your bills, keep you lookin' good, and take you and your kidz in, and fuck the shit out of you whenever you want, you better jump on it. Look, girl, I'ma tell you like this: ain't nobody says you gotta marry that muthafucka Raz, but use the shit out of him till you ready to move on to the next big thing. Ain't no need in feeling bad about it. Men was put on this earth for women to use the fuck up and discard. Shit, you been with that fuckin' no-job-havin' muthafucka Kelly since high school, and his broke ass ain't did nothing for you. Shit, he ain't even got you pregnant. Impotent bastard. The nigga ain't got no drive, no ambition or nothing. Girl, leave that nigga and get with somebody that can at least keep you laced up. And don't take too long to do it 'cause please believe you ain't the only bitch that's trying to get in with Raz. You just the one he has his sights set on." *For now anyway,* Twist thought.

Two hours later, it was dark as shit on the streets of West Philly, with all the broken streetlights and all.

"Kelly, I'm headed out. Don't wait up."

"Yo, Shan, hold up."

"What? I'm late!"

"Late for what? Going to the fuckin' clubs? Yo, that shit can wait. Come here."

"What? Kelly, I gotta go!"

"Not right the fuck now, you don't. Shit, girl, you lookin' real fuckin' fine right now. Seems like I only get to see you dressed up and lookin' all fine in passin' you on the way out. Come here, I need dat."

"What? I gotta goooo—" "Shhhhiiiittttt!" Shan yelled to herself as Kelly pulled her to him and started to tongue her down. At first she resisted, but then she realized that her bra was undone, and what's this? Her pussy was pounding and starting to drip. She hadn't felt this way in a long time. Not toward her husband at least.

"Damn it, girl! I'm tired of waitin' for you to stop frontin' and give me what's mine!" exclaimed Kelly as he sucked on her mouth even harder while removing her clothes and his.

In no time, they were both naked, and now the fun began. It'd been over a month, and Kelly's dick was hard as a motherfucka. Shan's pussy was now dripping wet, and Kelly's dick knew it, as if it could sense it, wanting more than anything to enter her now and shoot his hot load all up in her, but Kelly kept his cool while at the same time causing Shan to lose hers.

From standing to lying on the couch now, Kelly worked his magic, kissing Shan in all the right places—on her lips to her neck, moving down to those big juicy breasts, sucking like a starving newborn. Shan couldn't contain her moans of pleasure, which only drove him on to sucking on one, then the other, then both at once, moving down to her hot, dripping pussy and sucking on her clit nice and hard like she liked it.

"Owwwww yeah, baby, harder, harder!" she exclaims. She busted so hard, he damn near drowned down there.

Not one to be outdone, Shan now wanted that big dick in her mouth. And she went to work, sucking and sucking hard and fast. Kelly knew he could only take so much if it. Shan's head game was like no other, and he would bust soon if he let her continue. Sucking and slurping, moans of pleasure coming from both of them. Then he stopped her before it ended to soon, grabbed her, flipped her over, and started to eat out her ass as if it was his last meal, sucking and sliding up and down in and out her asshole and pussy.

Shan busted again. He made her bust one more time before she got on top of him and she rode that long fat shaft like a pro. "Oh shit, oh shit! I'm cummin' again!" she said.

"Oh shit, I'm cummin' with you!"

"Oooohhhh, *aaaaaaaaahhhhhhhhh! Shhhhhhiitttttttt!*" they both yell as they cum together. *Damn!* They both think at the same time.

Shan then vocalized, "We haven't cum together like that since we first got married."

"Yeah, I know. It's been too damn long, Shan. I mean, what the fuck, when we first got married, we would fuck like rabbits. Even after the kids came along, we was still getting it in damn near every day, three to four times. Now, nothing. You know I need dat. And I know you been fiendin' too, so what's been going on? And please don't tell me it's just because I haven't had a job in over a year. 'Cause I know we better than that."

Shan didn't say a word to that comment, but her facial expression spoke volumes. She wanted to tell Kelly he was a no-job-havin' muthafucka who just doesn't do it for her anymore. She wanted to tell him that he hadn't fucked her right since he lost his job (till tonight anyway). She wanted to tell him she was leaving him for another man whom she had been fucking for the past six months and taking her kids with her. She also wanted to tell him the kids weren't his.

But now her mind was more confused than ever, so what she said was "No, boo, it's not that, but it seems ever since you lost your job, you haven't been the same. And you just haven't touched me the same either, like all of a sudden, I repulse you or something. It's like lately, all you wanted to do was hop on, bust *your* nut, and hop off, and fuck how I feel. So you tell me, boo, what's up with that?"

That's it, girl, Shan thought. *Switch all this shit back around on this nigga. Make him feel real bad and low so when I decide to be out, he will know why and can't say shit 'cause he will know it was him that fucked us up. And I'll walk away smelling like roses.*

"Naw, baby—"

Here it comes. The bullshit excuses, she thought.

"—it ain't like that. It ain't like that at all, boo. You know you and them kids of ours mean the world to me. And I'm sorry if I made you feel some type of way. I know I ain't been myself, but I'ma get my shit together again. Just hang in there with me you'll see."

Gotcha, nigga. As Kelly pulled Shan toward him and they embrace, Shan smiled to herself. *Yeah, nigga. I gots you now.*

CHAPTER 5

Scandalous *Bitches*

Club, my ass! This was nothing more than a raggedy-ass bar. And that's putting it mildly. Nothing more than a fuckin' hole in the wall where hood ratz and wannabe ballers hang out to drink and pick out who they gonna fuck for the evening. This was Shan's idea of a club anyway—that's what she kept tellin' her husband. Two more hours went by while Twist and Raz waited on Shan to show, but she never did.

Needless to say, Raz was a little disappointed. Shan was some of the best pussy he has ever had, and he was looking forward to getting all up in dat tonight, but tonight was Kelly's time to be all up in it, and Raz would just have to wait his turn. Twist, on the other hand, was not so disappointed (not that she didn't love hanging out with her baby sis), but she had something else on her mind tonight.

"Damn, girl, where da fuck your sister at?" exclaimed Raz.

"Shit, I don't know!" said Twist. "In her skin, I guess, or maybe she found something better to do."

"What the fuck is dat supposed to mean? She know I be waitin' here on her and she be havin' a good fuckin' coming her way tonight. What better den dat?"

"Well, I ain't one to gossip, but you know, she is married. Maybe her husband said she couldn't go out tonight, or maybe—"

"Maybe what? Speak!"

"Oh, I don't know. Maybe she decided it was his turn to get in them skins tonight."

"*What!* Bullshit! She don't be wantin' that limp-dick muthafucker no more. She got a real mon in me now."

"All I'm sayin', Raz baby, is maybe—just maybe—there is a reason she hasn't left him yet."

"*Fuck,* dat some bumbaclot-fuckin' bullshit"

Yeah, muthafucka! Hold on to that image for a while, Twist thought to herself. *Yeah! Needs to get me some of that cream Shan been tellin' me about too. Shit, we sisters. We can share.*

The next day at D's crib, D was out on a hustle while Rock was still hidin' out at the crib. Kids were at school and Tracy was off from work.

"Shit, why D leave me up in here with that crazy fool?" Tracy said to herself. *"He knows I can't stand that nigga. I wish he would hurry and go back to wherever the fuck he came from. Well, guess I'll clean up a little while I'm off. Just hope that fuckin' nigga don't say shit to me."*

"Ninety-six, ninety-seven, ninety-eight, ninety-nine, one hundred."

"What the fuck did you do to my living room, Rock?"

"One, two, three, one. One, two, three, two. One, two, three, three. What, girl? You see me workin' out. I had to move the furniture a little out the the way. What's the problem?"

"The problem is—" As Tracy started to tell Rock the fuck off, she found she was a little stuck.

When she came downstairs, Rock was finishing some push-ups and started some three-count sit-ups. It wasn't till just this very moment that she noticed how built Rock really was—I mean, he was a fuckin' specimen. D was built and really cut, but Rock got about one hundred pounds on D, and all of it muscle. At one point in time, Tracy really had a weakness for big muscular guys like Rock—I mean, when I say weakness, I mean Tracy was a fuckin' ravenous whore when it came to guys like Rock. But she couldn't stand Rock's guts, and every time he came around, he wore really baggy clothes, so she never knew he had a body like that.

"Never mind," Tracy said as she caught herself. *Oh my god! I hope Rock didn't catch me slippin' like that,* Tracy thought as she walked toward the kitchen.

"Whatever, girl," said Rock as he continued his workout, thinking, *Yeah, girl, I saw that shit. You don't hate me that fucking much after all.*

Chapter 6

Gotcha, Bitch

"Okay, okay, I said I'm sorry, baby," Shan whispers as Raz is yelling in the phone on the other end.

"What you mean you couldn't get out last night? What! Now all of a sudden, your bumbaclot husband more important dan me?" His thick accent is showing through. "I should come over there an' sho' hem who your real man is."

"Please, baby, no!" Shan begs. "I promise, I will see you tonight." Shan calms Raz down with that and hangs up the phone. Good thing too. Despite all his money, Shan knows in a street fight, Kelly would tear Raz out the frame.

Shan starts to remember back when they were dating, some fool standing on the corner with two of his homies thought it would be a good idea to call her out her name while they were walking by. He paid for his lapse in judgment with a broken jaw. When his friends jumped in, they received the same treatment. Right then and there, she fell in love.

Just then, Kelly enters the room. "Who was that on the phone, babe?"

"No one. Just Twist wondering what happened to me last night," she lies. "I told her I would come out with her tonight and make it up to her."

"Okay,!" says Kelly. "Have fun. Since the kids are at your mother's and you're going out. I'ma go hang wit' D. I'll see you later."

"Okay, bye, babe," she says, thinking, *This works out great.*

Meanwhile, outside, Kelly makes a call on his cell.

"Yo, D! I'm on my way to your crib. Get ready. We need to roll out. I'ma need you to load them gunz for me tonight."

Ten minutes later, Kelly pulls up to D's crib. By this time, it's really starting to show on his face just how mad he is. D jumps in the passenger seat and doesn't say a word, but his actions speak volumes as he passes Kelly two big black Glock 45s with fully loaded clips and one in the pipe on each, twenty-two shots total, not to mention the S&W 40 that D is packing. The Glocks belong to Kelly, but he gave them to D sometime ago, back when the kids started walking. To Kelly's surprise, Rock is in tow and jumps in the backseat.

Kelly turns and speaks. "I don't know how it's gonna go down with your sister, Rock! And I makes no promises about nothing, so if you gonna feel some type of way about it, well, settle up after. Just don't get in it. And as for that Rasta nigga, he's done. And any of his homies that want it."

Rock replies, "Handle ya business. As for the Rastas, we got ya on dat shit!"

Twenty minutes go by, and Kelly, D, and Rock pull up to the bar. Before they could make a move, out comes Shan and Raz acting all cozy along with Twist and some nigga she picked up tonight.

She almost senses the slap coming before she feels it, and down she goes. Kelly socks the shit out Raz and backhands Shan in almost the same flawless motion. Before she hits the ground, she knows what had happened. Kelly must have picked up the phone while she was talking to Raz earlier, probably heard it all. Left the house all calm and cool like nothing happened just to get D (and probably his guns), but most of all, he just had to see it for himself so there could be no doubt.

Damn, bitch, Shan thinks. *You really fucked this shit up. Shit! Well, nothing to do but let this shit play out now.*

So it begins! "Muthafucka, who the fuck you layin' yo fuckin' handz on, nigga?" Shan yells.

"Yeah, nigga, who do you think you are?" Twist chimes in. *Pop* comes the slap to Twist, but not from Kelly. It's Rock who steps in to Kelly's surprise.

"Shut the fuck up, Twist!" yells Rock. "You fuckin' bitches embarrass me out here, acting like a couple of hoes."

Now there's a little crowd starting to gather outside.

"Twist, I expect this shit from you, but, Shan, you really surprise me," says Kelly.

Now Shan has managed to get back to her feet. "I surprise you? I surprise you? Muthafucka, ain't nobody out here more surprised than me of you. Shhiiiittt!" Spitting out some blood from the slap, Shan then proceeds to tear into her husband. "How long it's been, Kelly, since you had a fuckin' job, huh?

How long it's been since you was a fuckin' man, Kelly? How the fuck long, huh? How long since you fucked me right—?"

Pop! (she had to know that was comin) comes the slap that puts her right back on her ass. But she is on a roll now, no turning back. "Fuck you, nigga, don't be mad 'cause I done put your lame ass out in the streets now. At least Raz can lace me and my kids up and fuck me right. Oh, and by the way, muthafucka, the kids ain't yours!"

That last comment sent Kelly right over the edge, but he didn't go crazy and start shooting up the place like he originally planned to do. No, I think right there, right at that moment, he went truly (and not to beat a case but . . .) truly insane. This was where it started. He started smiling.

Raz was still on the ground, knocked out. The nigga who was with Twist didn't want no part of this drama and bounced the minute Raz hit the ground. Nobody in the crowd wanted no part of this either. They just wanted to watch these crazy-ass niggas show out. So Twist and Shan was on their own.

Shan then started talking shit to her brothers. "How the fuck can you fuckin' bastards take this muthafucka's side over mine? I'm your fuckin' flesh and blood! This nigga ain't shit to y'all"

Before D could answer, K-Block intercedes and hands him the keys to the car and tells him to open the trunk. Still smiling, he grabs Raz by the ankle and drags him to the car. He instructs D and Rock to hold him up. Still groggy, Block hit Raz in the guts, instantly waking him up. Block pulls one of his 45s and gives a shout-out to Shan and Twist. Pointing to them, he says, "I dedicate this to these two bitches who spend a lot of time, if not most of the time, on their knees!" *Bang, bang!* Block points and shoots out both of Raz's kneecaps.

"Aaaaaaaaaaaaaaaaaaaaaaaggggggggggggggghhhhhhhhhhhh!" Raz screams in pain.

"No, oh! No, don't scream yet, my friend. That was only your knees you won't be needing." Block snickers. "Knee-ding! Get it? You won't need them anymore. Not where you're going. And besides, your knees won't be the last thing I shoot off you tonight. Put him in the trunk."

"No, please, no!" Raz's begging and screaming fall on deaf ears.

Shan and Twist look on in disbelief. The crowd has run off at the first sign of gunfire, and now comes the sirens. Block tells D to start the car as he walks over to Shan. She is still on the ground, not believing what she is seeing.

K-Block kneels down. "As of now, me and you are done. Be out of my house by the time I get done with your friend, or I will end you, bitch. And if you think I'm joking, know that I will kill your fat-ass sister here right in front of you before I do you. I never want to see you again. Leave my kids at your mother's and get out of town tonight." Block then stands, turns, and jumps into the car, and they speed off.

Shan and Twist are still in disbelief.

"Yo, Block, you all right, bro?" says D.

"Never better," Block replies, still with that smile on his face.

"Yo, what we gonna do wit' the bleeding Rasta in the trunk, then?" says D.

"I know a place in the bottoms, nice and quiet," says Rock.

"Good!" Block replies. "Take us there. I'm gonna have me some fun with this nigga, and I wanna take my time doing it. Oh, and by the way, D?"

"What's up, my nigga?" asks D.

K-Block simply replies, "It's time."

CHAPTER 7

PCO (Paper Chaser Organization)

"Yo, D!"

"'Sup, Rock?"

"Dher go that nigga right there!"

"Oh, yeah! I see that muthafucka."

No sooner than that was said, their coal-black 745 BMW pulls up on the corner of Fifty-First and Market Street, next to a well-built young black man and two very menacing-looking bodyguards who had to each be pushing about three hundred pounds of muscle apiece. Down goes the tinted windows, and Rock shouts "**PCO, muthafucka!**" and unleashes with the twin SIG Sauers 40-cals, instantly dropping the two bodyguards and hitting the young black man in the leg before he could start running. Rock then jumps out onto the recently crowded intersection as D pops the trunk. "What the fuck, nigga? You thought we was playin'? We told you, nigga: you wanna push weight in this muthafuckin' town, you gots to cut PCO in or get the fuck cut out. Now I gotta take you to see da man."

"Noo, nooo, nooo, Rock, man, please, please, not the trunk! Not the trunk!"

Slam! is all you hear as the trunk lid closes. "Yo, D, man, I almost feel sorry for dat nigga," says Rock.

"Fuck you mean? Feel sorry! For what, nigga? These muthafuckas out here know what the fuck time it the fuck is. Yo, six months ago, we gave all these niggas notice. Fuck all the bullshit, PCO is running Philly point blank, period."

"You know I know, nigga. On the real, you know I could give a fuck about these niggas out here. Niggas know Rock will run down on any muthafucka out here without a second thought, and niggas know that I put mad work the fuck in. Even with all that, though, ya man is on some real other-level shit."

"Fuck you mean, nigga, *my* man? Block is as much my fuckin' brother as you are, and on the real, if it wasn't for him, we wouldn't be where we are right now, running this muthafucking city."

"I feel you, nigga, I feel you. But you know like I know, what he do to these niggas that cross us is un-fuckin'-real. Remember what the fuck he did six months ago to that fuckin' Rasta?"

"Yeah, nigga, I remember," says D.

"But, fuck it, he had it coming."

"On the real, I love that nigga Block like I love you, my brother, but damn, ya mean."

"Just drop it, Rock. Block do what Block do, and because of it, very few niggas even think about crossing us in this game. But every now and again, an example has to be made of. And the nigga in the trunk, his number just came the fuck up."

"I feel you, nigga. I feel you. But this time, one of them young niggas at the spot gonna have to clean up the mess."

The black BMW drives for about another twenty minutes, heading toward North Philly. It gets off Girard, heads to one of PCO's properties on Diamond Street. The BMW stops in front of a run-down old three-story reddish-brown-looking house. Even though there are people out on their stoops, kids running up and down the street, they all act like they see nothing when D and Rock open the trunk and pull the bleeding young black man from it and head into the house. The guard at the door instantly recognizes who they are, and before they can get up the steps good, the door swings open. They drag the young man in screaming and pleading, but it falls on deaf ears from inside and outside the house. They drag the young man kicking and screaming down a long hallway till they come to a big metal door. Any fool can instantly tell this door is not a part of the original architecture.

D knocks twice, and a slide on the door opens. Another man looks out to see who it is then instantly opens the door. Once through the door, they head down into the basement area of this old house. In this area, the walls are soundproof. The floor is wet, with drains embedded in it. There are chains with big sharp metal hooks hanging from the ceiling. There is a wall with all types of tools and knives hanging from it in a neat and orderly fashion. In the middle of the room, there is a metal table about the size of three operating tables with leather straps and chain restraints attached to it.

They drag the young man to the table. He screams louder and tries to resist even more with he sees the table and the tools on the wall. Rock hits him hard on the jaw, calms him right down, and actually knocks him out. They strap the leather restraints to his chest and upper thighs. By this time, they have removed every stitch of clothing he had on. The metal restraints are attached to his wrists and ankles. By the time they are done, the young man is strapped with his arms out to his side, like in a cross position, and his legs are spread-eagle. For now he's sleeping like a baby.

When they are finished, they head back upstairs and out to the other side of the door, where the guard who let them in follows them out and locks the door behind them.

"Yeah, torture, muthafucka!"

"Torture, nigga, what!"

The young black man strapped to the table starts to come out of his haze. He is awakened to the sounds of the Wu-Tang Clan's *Enter the Wu-Tang (36 Chambers)*.

"I fuckin', I fuckin' tie you to a fuckin' bedpost wit' yea ass cheeks spread out and shit right, put a hanger on a fuckin' stove and let that shit sit their for like a half hour take it off and stick it in ya ass slow like. *Sssssssssssssss!*

By this time, the young black man is fully awake and has returned to the panic he was previously in, yelling and screaming for help, but no one hears him except for the man who has slipped into the room through the door behind him. He doesn't notice the man who has been in the room since this almost prophetic song started to play, and he continues not to even sense the man in the room until he starts to speak right in sync with the last part of the intro to Method Man's song.

"I fuckin', I fuckin' sew ya asshole closed and keep feedin' you and feedin' you and feedin' you!" says K-Block as the music continues to play, and he walks over toward the tools hanging on the wall, right past the young man strapped to the table, as if he doesn't even see him.

Seeing who it is in the room with him, the young man begins to plead for his life. "Block! Please, Block, don't do this. I didn't mean any disrespect toward you or the PCO, man. I was just trying to get my paper out there. Please, please, please, Block! Please! Just give me another chance. I will make it up to you, man. I will give you twice—no, no, no—three times what anyone else pays."

As if in a trance, Block continues what he was doing, as if the young man was not even in the room. Block continues to look over the various instruments hanging on the wall and some laid out on a workbench.

Hammers and screwdrivers of all shapes and sizes, chisels, drills and various bits, axes, sledgehammers, chainsaws. Knives of all types, metal shears, pliers—the list goes on and on. He picks up a Bowie knife of good size (at least a six-inch blade), looks it over, then starts to sharpen it with the power grinder mounted on the other end of the workbench.

Seeing what is going on, the young man begins to beg some more, and with good reason. It wasn't just the fact he was strapped down and helpless and left to the mercies of a well-known psychopath. No. Ya see, he knows who Block is and what he is capable of. In fact, everyone in the city of Philadelphia knew. And just like everyone else, he knew just what happed to Raz six months ago.

CHAPTER 8

Torture

Six months earlier . . .

If you had told this Rasta nigga Raz that by 12:00 a.m. on this evening, he would be in the trunk of an old Buick with both kneecaps shot out, crying like a baby, and fearing for his life, he would have never believed you. You see, the RazMon, or Raz for short, was not a slouch in the game to say the least. In a time when every drug dealer in the game was trying to become king of the streets, Raz was already at the very least a prince. He ran his own drug business out of Southwest Philly. He had like two hundred to three hundred workers on the streets running and dealing, about fifteen drug houses all over Philly, not to mention the fourteen strip clubs and sixteen bars he owed (all drug fronts). He also had a piece of the prostitution game, as well as four or five legitimate businesses like car dealerships and day cares.

Yeah, he was pretty big and well-known on these streets, so if you had told him that some fuckin' nobody from fuckin' nowhere would have him fearing for his life, he would have thought you crazy.

And that's just what K-Block was, a nobody. Raised in a good home—not a rich home or anything like that but maybe middle class. His parents were good people who raised their two children right. Taught them to believe in God and themselves.

Tonight K-Block would take all those lessons, distort them, and use them for his own dark designs.

Driving the old Buick down the street, Block thought, all the while still smiling, *It pays to listen to your instincts. I knew that bitch was foul. Them kids ain't even mine, and somehow I knew. Not their fault though. Can't blame them.*

But that bitch! That fuckin' bitch! She knew all along and played me like a fuckin' fool. Played my heart, my soul. Took the best years of my life. Fuckin' whore. Heh! It's all good, though. I ain't even that mad at her. Fuck that dirty bitch now. All those months making me feel like shit. Fuck her. She will live, if only to see what she has unleashed in me and on this fuckin' city. Hope she leaves town, though. I will kill her and her whore-ass sister right in front of her if she stays.

"Yo, Block, turn here," says Rock from the backseat, interrupting Block's train of thought. "Go down two more blocks. See the vacant lot? There is an old run-down house right on the other side with nobody around."

"Cool, I see it. This is gonna be fun." K-Block slows down the car and pulls up in the vacant lot right behind the old house. Fortunately there are a few beat-up, burned-out wrecks in the area, so no one will notice one more fucked-up Buick. "Check this out," says Block. "I need a minute in the house. When I come out, all I need is for you two to keep watch. I'll deal with this muthafucka myself."

"Cool," they both reply.

Block steps out of the car and checks the house. Prime location and boarded-up house like this is just a haven for squatters and crackheads to get high in. But Block was in no mode for either. Luckily, the house was clear because tonight had he ran across either, they would have been shot on sight. When he finished searching the house, he returned to the car. "D, pop it," says Block.

For a split second, Raz thinks he can escape if he rushes Block, but that second soon passes as he sees the .45 pointed and ready, and he remembers the pain he is having from the two holes in his knees.

Time to get the fuck out, nigga, Block thinks as he grabs him with his free hand and lets him drop to the ground with a thud. Block pulls some rope from the trunk hands it to Rock. "Tie this nigga's hands behind his back." Block then grabs him by one of his legs and pulls him into the house. Dragging him like a sack of shit, Block pays no regard to the glass and nails and various other debris on the ground and all over the house's floors. Right through the front door, through the living room, dining room, to the kitchen down the stairs, and he doesn't care in the least that Raz's head bounces off all twelve steps till it hits the cement basement floor and knocks him back out. Tucking his gun into its holster, he grips up the Rasta and throws him onto an old workbench in the middle of the room. As it happens, this basement looks as if it was someone's old woodshop at one point in time. Block is loving this. He unties his hands and places the barely conscious Raz's hands into two old vises and tightens them. The first one he tightens just enough to hold him in case he wakes up. The second one he goes full bore and tightens it till he starts to hear bone crack and thus consequently wakes Raz.

"Aaaaaaaaaaaaahhhhhhhhhhhhhhhhhh!" Raz screams in pain.

Now that I have your attention, time for the other hand, Block thinks, as he tightens the first vise. Raz's screams are like music to Blocks ears, and tonight, he is playing a symphony.

K-Block has really, really lost it, and he doesn't care. He looks over to the old shelving and particle board where tools were once hung and sees an old rusty wood saw a pair of pliers and an old hammer. He smiles more. He grabs the instruments and lays them neatly on the countertop next to the workbench. Block then reaches under his coat and pulls out a very large survival knife. Raz's eyes widen at the sight of it. Then, for the first time since they met tonight, K-Block speaks to him.

"You know, I should thank you. If you hadn't been fucking my wife, I would have never known what a whore she was. So thank you." *Slam!* The knife made the sound as it hit the table, passing through Raz's right knee in the exact spot he was shot, sticking him now and stapling him to the wooden bench. But you wouldn't have noticed the sound of the knife over Raz's screams.

"Now the fun really begins," says K-Block as he moves in with the rusty saw he laid on the counter. He starts in the left leg, cutting just below the knee. Back and forth he goes with the saw as Raz's screams go unheard. "Shut the fuck up, bitch. We just getting started," says K-Block as he finishes with the leg. "Shut up and hold this," he says, only half-joking as he tosses the severed leg to Raz. But with his hands crushed in the vises, it lands on his chest and sits there. He screams louder.

He then grabs the old pliers and starts on the toes, pulling out all five of Raz's remaining toenails, saying all the while, "This little piggy went to market, and this little piggy stayed home. This little piggy had roast beef, and this little piggy had none, and this little piggy went 'Wee, wee, wee' all the way home."

Block is having the time of his life as he goes once again for the saw. Now Raz is begging, pleading, whimpering for his life. Block hears none of this as he goes for the right arm with the saw. Raz sees it coming again, and as the cutting begins, so do the screams until he passes out from the loss of blood and trauma.

"Oh no! Oh no! Not yet. You can't die yet," says Block. He quickly removes and shreds Raz's clothes and makes quick tourniquets around where Raz's arm and leg used to be and stops the flow of blood just enough to revive him. "No, no, no, my man. You can't die yet. Just one question before you go, and to make sure I have your attention."

Bam, bam, bam! goes the hammer into Raz's nuts. He can't even scream.

"How many times did you *fuck* my wife? Hmmmm?"

Raz cannot answer. His mouth has filled with blood, and he is choking on it. His lungs have started to collapse. He has lost way too much blood. The trauma to his body is too much. He is just about done.

"Can't answer huh? Well, let me answer that for you. **One fuckin' time too many!**"

Then it's lights out permanently for Raz as the hammer now crushes his skull.

Unbeknownst to K-Block, D and Rock had witnessed almost this whole unholy act being committed. The screams of Raz getting his leg removed had sent them running to see what was going on. They had thought Block would maybe beat him down some more and put a bullet in his head, but they never expected anything like this.

"I told you two to keep watch," says Block without even turning around, as if he sensed them there all of a sudden.

"Yo, Block, what the fuck did you do?" says D "What the fuck is this?" D questions.

"What the fuck is this? What the fuck is this? **This** is just the beginning!"

CHAPTER 9

9 mm

"You gotta know by now that you don't have enough money to buy your way out of this," says Block. "But I'll tell you what I'm gonna do. I'm feeling a little generous today. Your gonna die here today, ain't no avoiding that, but I'm gonna let you choose how."

"Please, Block, please," begs the young man.

"Please, you say? Please what, nigga? You wasn't saying 'Please can I come to your town and sell dope?' You didn't say 'Please may I disrespect you and your organization by pissin' on the standing order not to sell in this town without approval and tribute to the PCO?'"

"Please, Block, I'm sorry please," the young man emphatically begs.

"Please, please, I'm sorry, Block, pleaseeee," mocks K-Block. "Bullshit on that, nigga. Fuck you. You see, I was gonna let you take a bullet to the head. Pull out the nine and straight peel yo cap back, but now with all your bitchin' you got me in the mood for some fun. You was supposed to be a real G. Instead you a real *B* for 'bitch-ass nigga.' What? You thought I didn't know you was going to all the clubs and all the hot spots talking shit like you about to take over and run this town? Nigga, please! PCO runs Philly, and you just one more nigga that gots to be shown."

Bang! Down comes the knife into the young man's shoulder. And on cue come the screams. And as usual, K-block smiles.

Upstairs posted guards at the front door, two young men, carry on a conversation. "Yo, man, I'm glad D had all that soundproofing put in."

"Yeah, man, me too. I mean Block just didn't give a fuck who heard all them niggas screaming."

"Yeah, Block be on some ol' other level shit. Don't give a fuck about no jakes or nothing."

"Yeah, Block don't care. He know he run this town and damn near everything and everyone in it, po-po included."

"Yeah, nigga. Just glad it ain't me down there strapped to his fuckin' table."

"I feel you nigga. I definitely feel ya."

Just then, the two young men hear the big metal door down the long hallway open and slam shut. They see Block come toward them. They know the deed is done and another life has been extinguished at Block's hands.

"Get down their and clean that shit up," orders Block. "When you're finished, take that nigga and all his parts and dump him in the usual place. No wait! Dump that nigga wherever his crew hangs out. Gotta let these niggas know in case there is another one waiting in the wings. Where's D?"

"He's up in the office," replies one of the young men.

"Cool! Now get to that business and get back here fast. I got another job for you two."

CHAPTER 10

MOB

As K-Block enters the office on the third floor of the old house, he is greeted by the sounds of female moans, male grunts, and the smell of sex in the air. Once again, D and Rock are up in the office fucking the shit out of two fine-ass bitches, probably from one of PCO's strip clubs. D is piping the shit out of one bitch on the desk while Rock is up in the corner, holding up his bitch in the air, her legs straddling him while he pounds the shit out of her.

"I done told you niggas, stop fucking these bitches up in this here office. It's like five other rooms up here, and y'all two niggas wanna fuck in the office!" exclaims Block.

"Yo, Block," says D, "you know we just be on some spur-of-the-moment type shit an' we just fuck on site sometimes, you know?" exclaims D, not missing a beat pounding on his bitch's pussy.

"Yeah, you know how we do, Block," says Rock, not missing a stroke.

"Well, my niggas, come on up out the pussy time for business," says Block. Without missing a beat, both D and Rock stop in midstroke, pull up their pants, and dismiss the bitches who leave the room without a word. Block takes a seat behind the old wooden desk in the office—the same one D was just fucking on—and puts up his feet. "Okay, fellas, what we got?" says Block.

D responds "What we got is Philly on smash. We got West Philly locked, North Philly locked, Southwest locked, and most of South Philly locked."

"What's the problem with South Philly, Rock? You were supposed to have that shit under control by now," says Block.

Rock responds, "We still gots some niggas pushing weight without our say-so. Probably some of the Razta's old click. Once we took over Southwest they took over a little section of South Philly. They got them island connects that we ain't got to yet."

"So fucking kill the fucking dealers. You know the drill. What's the problem?"

"The problem is," says Rock, "that the muthafuckers ain't dealing on the corners or in the usual crackhouses. These niggas done got smart, and not only are they managing to dodge the cops, they dodging us at the same time and still pushing weight."

"So what you gonna do about it?" says D.

"What I'm gonna do about it is already being done. Got some workers on the streets now. Once they get back to me, and we know how they moving the product and where they hiding, I'll head down there with some of the boys and deal wit' them."

"Whatever you do, make it quick," says Block. "Can't have these niggas making money unauthorized for too long and we ain't getting a piece."

"You right!" Rock agrees.

"Other than that, do we have any other business?" says Block.

"Just one. Potential problem with the new police commissioner," replies D.

"What? You mean all that bullshit he been getting on the news talkin'?" says Block.

"Yeah!" replies D. "You know we had the last commissioner in our pocket, but this muthafucka won't be bought. This nigga act like he invincible or some shit. When I approached him with the payoff, this nigga was on some ol' 'I don't want your dirty blood money!' Talking like he all high and mighty and gonna put all of us under the jail and shit."

"D, don't even worry about that nigga. I already got something in the works for that fucker," says Block.

"You care to share, good brother?" asks D.

"All I will say is this, bro. I only deal with cops three ways: buy 'em, scare 'em, or kill 'em. The first two don't always work, but the third way is a surefire winner."

"Yo, Block, now its one thing to kill one of these uniformed beat cops, but the commissioner? You sure we want that type of heat coming down on us?" says D.

"Look, bro," says Block, "you trusted me this far even when you didn't always understand what the hell I was doing, and now look at us. We fucking run this city, and it's only been six months. In the next couple of months, we'll start looking to expand. New York, Jersey, Delaware, on and on. It don't stop. Six years from now, I plan on being the president's fucking dealer, ya feel me?"

"I feel ya, bro," replies D.

"Yo, now's not the time for us to worry about some new fucking top cop," says Block. "I'll have that nigga down in the basement just as quick as I would any other nigga. But what we need to make major moves is major players on our team from both sides of the law. And if it's one thing I've learned from all the niggas I done had in my workshop in the basement, it's that every man—every fuckin' man—has a breaking point or a weakness that can be exploited from the hardest rock to the weakest mark."

"You right!" Rock agrees.

"Now with that being said," says Block, "you two niggas gotta learn some fuckin' discipline."

"What you mean, Block?" says D.

"You know what the fuck I mean. I'm talking about these bitches you two keep bringing up in through here. Don't get me wrong. I loves pussy as much as the next man—in fact, more. But there is a time and a place. You niggas don't seem to get that shit."

"Awh! Come on, Block!" says Rock.

"'Awh! Come on,' nothing. Look, we living large right now, and we gotta look to the future and all that shit, but just 'cuz we on top don't mean somebody ain't waiting in the wings to take us down, and all they need to do it is a weakness that they can exploit. You niggas running to the clubs and strip joints every chance you get for some pussy. Eventually, somebody gonna notice that as your weakness and use it against you. Against us. Mightier men than you two have been taken down and taken out due to the power of the P. Don't forget that shit. One minute you fucking some bitch in the back of the club, and the next, you lying on the floor with your fucking brains leaking out. Remember, my niggas, we gotta be MOB all the time, and niggas gotta know it, they gotta see it, and they gotta feel it, dig me?"

"You right, Block," says D. "No doubt, money over bitches at all times, my nigga. You is definitely right," D says.

"I feel you, my nigga," says Rock. "I feel you."

CHAPTER 11

Horse

Two hours later, after some more discussion on the state of business and expansion, Block asks, "Yo, D, you still cool with that cop that drives the commissioner around?"

D replies, "Yeah, man. That's my nigga. Why?" D can see the wheels turning in K-Block's head. He's seen that look on his face before.

Without answering, Block opens the top drawer of the old wooden desk he's been sitting behind, pulls out some paper and a Sharpie, and starts writing. When he stops, he looks at his work and smiles.

Just then, there is a knock on the door. The two young men Block sent to dump the body earlier have returned. They announce themselves and enter the room. These two young bulls, about seventeen and eighteen respectively, are new to the PCO, still earning their stripes in the crew, and they are hungry and loyal, just like K-Block likes, but they still have to prove themselves to Block before being put in any real position of power. Right now, these two youngbloods named Low and Dirty are more or less just errand boys. Ya know, they do the corner work and the mule work, etc.

The younger of the two, Low, speaks, "Yo, Block, you should have seen the faces of them niggas when we rolled up and started throwin' the pieces of they mans out the car. Them niggas was like 'Oh shit! Oh shit! What the fuck? What the fuck is this! Oh shit!' Ha-haaaa! Them niggas was running and crying and bitchin' all at the same time. That was some funny shit."

Then Dirty chimes in "Yeah, man, that shit was funny as hell! One nigga got hit in the face with one of the nigga's arms an' shit and fell down. When he sat up, he was screamin' like a bitch when he realized what the fuck it was he was holdin'."

Low and Dirty are already cracking up when Block, D, and Rock get a picture of that scene in their heads, and they start crackin' up too.

When they all stop laughing, Low says, "So what else you got for us, Block?"

Right down to business. Block liked that but didn't let the young bull know it. *Gotta keep niggas hungry and striving for approval.* "You know where the horse stables are in the park?" says Block.

"Yeah! Out there on Chamounix Road right?" says Low.

"Yeah," says Block. "I need you to get something for me out there tonight and deliver it somewhere." Block then raises the note so that D and Rock can now read it.

They both smile, and without saying a word, D pulls out his cell and makes a call. "About nine thirty till twelve o'clock. Cool, that's good-lookin', my nigga," says D into the phone before hanging up. "About ten o'clock tonight would be good, Block," says D.

"Cool, that will work," Block replies. He then turns to face the two young bloods waiting for orders. Block speaks. "Now here's what I need you to do."

After receiving their orders, Low and Dirty jump into one of the many black BMW 745s owned by the PCO—all bulletproof and all with a ton of weapons stashed in them. Driving down the street, Dirty speaks. "Yo, Block is crazy man. Only he would come up with so ol crazy ass shit as this."

"Yo, shut the fuck up nigga. Block's the fuckin' man. What he says goes, nigga. Don't forget that shit," says Low.

"Yo, chill, nigga. I ain't sayin' he ain't the man, and the deed will definitely get done, no doubt. But I'm just sayin'—"

"Shut the fuck up nigga," Low cuts him off. "I don't care what you saying. Keep ya mind on the business at hand. This is the most responsibility that Block has ever given us. This is big, and we can't afford no screwups. So just shut the fuck up and drive."

Twenty minutes later, Low and Dirty arrive at their destination. They jump out of the car, and Low pops the trunk and grabs the chain saw he put back there before they left. They head inside the building. "Yo, Low, which one?"

"That big white one right there," says Low.

Pop, pop, pop! goes the sound of Dirty's chrome nine. Then it's Low's turn with the chainsaw he brought. After collecting their package in a big Hefty bag, they roll out.

"Yeah, D, it went real smooth," says Low in his cellphone. "We on our way to drop off the package now."

Thirty minutes after the phone call to D, Low and Dirty arrive at their destination. They move real quiet-like to the back through an open window, up the rear stairs in the kitchen so as not to alarm or awake anyone. They hear the TV on in the next room and some female laughing but pay her no mind. She is unaware that they are even there. They arrive at their destination, the master bedroom. Then pull back the covers of the fresh linen bed and remove their cargo from the Hefty bag and place it in the middle of the bed. Low pulls out a knife given to him just for this job and a note that he staples to the package with the knife. They then pull the covers up per their instructions and leave the same way they came in, still undetected. They head back to the car, which was parked not too far away, and calmly and casually drive away.

Low pulls out his phone and dials. "The deed is done. We're heading back now," says Low.

"Good," says D on the other end. "Block," says D, "the package has been delivered."

"Good," says Block. "Now we watch and wait."

A little while later, Low and Dirty return. They report right to the office where Block and D are waiting.

"Did you do everything to the letter as I instructed?" says Block.

"To the letter," Low replies.

"Were you seen by anyone?" says Block.

"No one," responds Dirty.

"Cool, then here, catch." Block tosses each of them a stack of cash with fifties and one-hundred-dollar bills, a total of $4,000 apiece. "Now here's what you two gonna do now. Head down to the Pic on Allegany. I made a call. Tonight you gonna drink what you wanna drink, smoke what you wanna smoke, and fuck who you wanna fuck. On me. And be back here tomorrow by five o'clock p.m. Dig me?"

Low and Dirty are struck. They never really thought about getting paid for the job they did. They thought it was just another deed to be done to earn their stripes, but getting paid and laid and high all on K-Block, they never would have dreamed. They both thank Block and run out of there before he changes his mind, both of them anticipating the night ahead.

"Gotta keep them loyal, huh, Block?" says D.

"Loyalty is a funny thing, D. It goes both ways. Even a boss has to show loyalty to his troops, or else they start wondering what they loyal to him for." Block replies.

"I feel ya, big bro, but these young niggas. You sure you ain't give them too much too fast?" says D.

"Come on, D," says Block. "You know me better than that. To us that was just chump change. What I gave them tonight wasn't no real money, only eight Gs. And shit, them having a good time at the Pic, that ain't nothing when you own the place. But two young, ruthless, and hungry niggas loyal only to us, nigga, that's priceless."

The next day, it was business as usual. Niggas in the trap selling that product and collecting that paper. Bitches on the corner selling that ass and collecting that cash. Low and Dirty are right back at it on their usual corner, handling business. Around four forty-five, Dirty checks his watch and motions to Low that it's time. After securing the product in the stash spot and letting the other niggas working for PCO in the area know that they are about to roll, Low and Dirty head down the block to the old house Block told them to report to at five o'clock. Once in the house, they report to the office where Block, D, and Rock have just turned on the big sixty-two-inch plasma hanging on the wall and are watching the channel 6 five o'clock news.

"And the big story today on *Action News!*" says the anchorman on the TV. "Police commissioner Herbert Jackson's house was vandalized last night by an unknown party. We take you live to the scene." The reporter at the scene continues the report, saying that the police have no leads or clues to the whereabouts or, for that matter, the identity of the person or persons who committed this heinous crime. They further detail the report by saying "that around midnight last night, Commissioner Jackson and his wife were returning from a benefit and entered the house. While the commissioner was in the process of paying their teenage babysitter, his wife, Mrs. Roberta Jackson went upstairs to check on their children, five- and six-year-old Kristen and Colin.

"After seeing that they were okay, she headed into the master bedroom where she found the gruesome discovery. She screamed, and the commissioner and the babysitter ran upstairs to find Mrs. Jackson passed out on the floor. While tending to his wife, the babysitter screamed, and the commissioner turned to see what it was she was screaming at and saw it—the severed head of a white horse that had apparently been shot several times and placed on the bed. It had been placed under the covers and had soaked the bed in its blood.

"The commissioner could not be reached for comment. Our sources indicate that Commissioner Jackson, his wife, and their two small children have been moved to a remote safe location pending investigation."

Block turns down the TV while the reporter still reporting. He looks over the desk at D and Rock, then he looks at Low and Dirty. Almost immediately they all started laughing.

After about five minutes of laughing and cracking jokes at the commissioner's expense, Block manages to pull himself together and says, "Now that's what the fuck I'm talking about. Now all we have to do is wait." Everyone in the room knows why even the young bloods know why. This fucking game is like chess. Everyone gets a turn. Block made his move. Now he has to wait for the commissioner to make his. Not only that, but everyone also noticed that no mention was made of the knife or the note.

CHAPTER 12

Next Move

"Herbert! Herbert! Herbert, wake up! Wake up!" exclaims Roberta.

"What! What is it, babe?" Herbert says in a very groggy voice.

"I hear something," says Roberta.

"Baby, it's been two weeks since we moved from the last safe house because you were hearing noises in the night. It's nothing, and if it were, I have guards posted around the clock. Nothing and nobody goes in or out of this house without my say-so. Now go back to sleep," says Herb.

"Well, I'm sorry, Herbert, that I'm not a hardened street cop turned commissioner with twenty years of service. I'm sorry that I don't have nerves of steel and that I can't look death and terror in the eye and laugh. I'm sorry, I'm just so sorry I'm just a scared little woman—scared to death for her children, her husband, and herself. I'm so, so sorry."

"Look, babe," a now wide awake Herb says, "I know all of that. I know you're scared, but you gotta trust that I won't let anything happen to you or the kids."

"But, sweetie, I do trust you. But what about the note? I know your reasons for not bringing it up to the press and all, but what are we gonna do? There is a psycho out there, and he has a reputation for not caring about the law or cops, and he has this family in his sights. Not to mention he has most of this city in his pocket," says Roberta.

"I know all that, baby, but we can't . . . I can't run from this, or this city or everyone in it is truly lost," says Herbert.

"I know, but I will not allow this city or your pride to put our family in danger. I think you should consider early retirement like we discussed, and we should get out of Dodge," says Roberta.

"Get outta Dodge?" exclaims Herbert. "'Get out of dodge,' you say. So your solution is that we should just run away? Let this asshole just run us out of our home, out of town just like that? And if we run, what about the next time we're pushed into a corner. Should we run again? And after that? We will never stop running if we start now. Why can't you understand that?"

"I do understand!" exclaims Roberta. "I just don't care. I don't care if we run today, tomorrow, or forever just as long as we are safe. Don't forget, I read that note too. I know what that madman's intentions are, and I have seen and heard what he is capable of, and damn this city to hell if you think that I won't leave and take the kids with me if you insist of staying here and fighting a war with a crazy man."

"*Leave?*" a now angry Herb shouts. "Nobody is leaving, Roberta! *Not* you, not *my kids*—*nobody*! So you might as well get that bullshit right out of your head. Where the fuck you think you would go, huh? To your sisters? Maybe your parents? Don't you know this fucking lunatic will go through you *and* the kids to get at me. That's how this guy works! *No rules, no boundaries, no fucking limits* to what he will do. How can I protect you and the kids if you leave? This muthafucka will kill everyone you come in contact with, everyone you love, just to use you to get to me. That's how he works. If you were scared before because of what you see in the news and what you hear in passing, just know that it isn't even a fraction of what this man is capable of. You don't see the police reports, the firsthand accounts from witnesses that all of a sudden go missing, or the fucking crime scenes this guy leaves behind. You don't know shit about this muthafucka, and he got you shook. So leaving, my dear, is out of the fucking question."

"Herb," says Roberta, now visibly shaken, "baby, now I'm really terrified because . . . because you sound like you might be a little afraid too."

Herb replies, "Baby . . . I am."

Two hours and a couple of sleeping pills later, Roberta is fast asleep. But not Herb, who has left their bedroom and is sitting in the den of their second safe house. *Not bad as safe houses go—four bedrooms, two baths, backyard, plenty of space. One of the perks of being the police commissioner in hiding, I guess.* Herb unlocks the top desk drawer in the den of his home office and removes two plastic bags one containing the knife used to pin a note to the horse's head and the other containing the actual note. He removes the note from its plastic bag and reads it for what seems like the thousandth time. It simply says "SO HOW'S THE FAMILY?" in big bold letters stained with the horses' blood.

Each time Herb reads this note, he instinctively runs to check on his children, just like he did that first night after reading this note. Standing in the doorway of his children's room, seeing they're okay, he thinks of all he has gone through in his police career. He has known fear. He has been shot, stabbed, and beaten, but still he managed to overcome it and rise to the top. But now standing here in the doorway, looking down on his children, he admits to himself that he has never known fear like this, and for the first time in his life, he doesn't know if he can overcome it. But he does know he can't run from it. He had already made up his mind long before, and if he wasn't sure then, he is sure now. He thinks, *If its war you want, muthafucker, it's a fucking war you will get.*

CHAPTER 13

Prepare for Battle

The next day, Herb is all business. He locks himself in his office and instructs his secretary to cancel and reschedule all his meetings for the week, including his one with the mayor. Herb knows the mayor is a sniveling coward and weakling, but he isn't sure if he is corrupt. Herb knows, of course, that he was a typical politician—just as corrupt as the rest—but what he doesn't know is whether the mayor is in the pockets of this madman he is about to go to war with. Either way, he doesn't have time to cater to the mayor's ego—not this week anyway. Too much to plan and too much at stake. And if the mayor is partnered with the enemy, then he too would be dealt with soon enough.

Herb's mind is racing a mile a minute. He has the makings of a plan—at least the start of one—and he wants to get right to it. First he would review the file of every officer under his command who is known to be a good, clean cop, incorruptible and untainted by the PCO. Herb knows his time is limited, and he knows he could not go over the file of every single officer on the Philadelphia police force, but he also knows even before he took this job just how far the PCO reached. So he actually started this plan well before he got the job and started reviewing files months ago. What he found was the good, clean, incorruptible officers he was looking for were in the minority. So finding what he was searching for would not take that long. When Herb first took this job, he figured he would just come in and clean up the PPD, but now the plan is survival of the fittest and of the most prepared.

The first part of Herb's plan would be to put together a sort of Eliot Ness Untouchables style of unit that he would use on the streets to shake things up a bit for the PCO. But the first part is starting to be the hardest part. Although the list of good offices is short, Herb finds that the majority of them are either about to retire and just trying to stay alive long enough to get their pension or just fresh out of the academy and have yet to be street tested. Although there were a few good candidates like Officer Juan Ramirez from the Nineteenth District, born and raised in North Philly; Officer Dwayne Morris out of the Twelfth District, born and raised in West Philly; and Officer Vanessa Lopez out of the Thirteenth, born in New York, moved to North Philly when she was six.

Still, we are gonna need a lot more good officers to make this work, Herb thought. *These officers are good and have been tested, but not long. Ramirez and Lopez only have five and six years in. Morris, the veteran of the group, at least has ten in, and he seems to have good leadership ability. I can use that, but more will be required.*

Can't call the Feds. Gonna have to call on some old friends.

Herb buzzes his secretary. "Jill!"

"Yes, Commissioner?"

"I need you to initiate a conference call for me with Chief Williams of the NYPD and Chief Hardbrook of the LAPD."

"Right away, sir!"

Time to call in some old favors, Herb thinks. *Some really big favors.*

Three hours later, the conference call ends between the three chiefs, and for the first time in weeks, Herb manages to crack a smile. *This could actually work.*

Herb grabs his hat and his coat and heads out the door. "Jill, I'm leaving for the day. See you tomorrow," says Herb.

"Yes, sir. Bright and early. Good night," says Jill.

"Good night."

Herb checks his watch—5:00 p.m. *Good, still early enough.* Herb removes his cell phone from his pants pocket as his police officer–driven car pulls up (one of the perks of being commissioner). He gets in and dials his wife. "Babe, I'm feeling good today," he says to her. "I hope you didn't cook dinner 'cause were going out. So get the kids ready. I'll be home in thirty minutes." He hangs up the phone and starts thinking again. *This could actually work. No, this will work. Can't wait to get started.*

Miles away, D is sitting in the backseat of one of the PCO's black Beamers, on his cell phone, having a very intense conversation with the person on the other end.

"What the fuck are you doing calling me like this? What, did you think a couple of months would pass and it would be all good again? Naw, bitch, you fucked that shit up real good," says D to the person on the other end of the phone. "Hell, no! Do I have to spell that shit out for you? You know what the fuck he is capable of. Can't say I blame him too much if you—"

D is cut off by the voice on the phone and is silent for a long moment. "Fine. Okay, I'll do it. I said I would fuckin' do it, but you listen to me. Things are not like you remember. Shit is a whole lot different, and I can't say I know how he will react and what the fuck he will do. He's not the same dude no more thanks to you. He might just kill you on sight, and I don't know if I can stop him—"

D is cut off again. "Fine, do whatever. I'll set it all up, but don't call me again. Good-bye, Shan."

Five minutes later, D instructs the driver of the Beamer to pull over to one of the PCO's money spots. Today it's D's turn to make the rounds and make sure business is running smooth. He hops out of the backseat and instructs the driver to keep the car running. He walks up to the door, and it immediately opens. He disappears inside.

Five seconds later, the driver of the Beamer is on his cell phone. "Yo, Block, this is Dirty. I got some info you might want to hear."

The week is moving at a lightning pace now for Herb. Everything is coming together according to his plan. He has now found, contacted, and assembled the officers from his entire department whom he needed, and they came from districts all over Philly. He has also contacted and assembled officers from New York and Los Angeles as a special task force under his command with permission from each of the cities' commissioners. And he was able to get all this done in the span of two weeks. *Now on to phase 2,* thinks Herb as he rings for his secretary. "Jill?"

"Yes, Commissioner?" Jill responds over the intercom.

"Reschedule my meeting with the mayor for Monday. Morning is preferable, and I need to speak to Captain Lewis from the police training academy."

"Yes, sir, right away," responds Jill.

After this meeting, I'll know where the mayor's loyalties lie, and I'll know how I'll have to deal with him, Herb thinks. *Yes, everything is going according to plan. Now I need some more intel on the enemy. That will be tricky.*

Just then, Herb's intercom rings, interrupting his train of thought. "Sir?"

"Yes, Jill?" says Herb.

"Sir, the meeting with the mayor has been set for eight o'clock a.m. Monday morning, and Captain Lewis from the training academy is on line 2."

"Thanks, Jill," says Herb as he picks up line 2. "Hello, Captain, how are you today? That's good. I won't take up too much of your time. I just have a couple of questions to ask you."

Monday morning at 8:00 a.m. sharp, Herb is sitting in the office of Mayor Wilson James, and as usual, the mayor is late. No worries though. Herb already knew when he set this meeting with the mayor that the man would intentionally come late.

For one thing, the mayor feels that he was the most important man in the world, or at least this city, and people should be waiting on him and not the other way around, so he always manages to show up just a little bit late for every meeting. Then he would arrive, as always with some lame excuse as to why. On his really bad days, he wouldn't even bother with an excuse or an apology and would just come in and start the meeting as if he didn't just have everyone waiting for him for the last twenty to thirty minutes. All of the mayor's executive staff know not to be late or, at the very least, not to arrive after him. Heaven forbid His Majesty should have to ever wait.

And the second reason Herb knows the mayor would be late, and perhaps the most important reason, is that Herb cancelled their last meeting, and no one cancels on Mayor James. For that insult, Herb will be waiting at least an hour.

But none of this matters to Herb if he could get what he wanted out of this meeting. And almost as Herb predicted, almost two hours later, in comes Mayor James. *Here comes the bullshit*, Herb thinks.

"Herb, sorry I'm late," says Mayor James. "I overslept and traffic was a bear."

"No problem, Wilson," Herb replies (lying through his teeth). "No problem at all. How was your weekend?" asks Herb.

"It was great. Me and the missus spent some long overdue quality time together. We went on over to Jersey to the beach and the casinos and had a blast. How about you?"

"Oh, it was fine. I don't want to take up too much of your time, Mayor. I know you're very busy. I really just have a request to ask of you."

"Oh! What is it?" asks Wilson.

"It is a request of two parts, really. The first part is, I need you to give the new cadets in the police training academy a little time off. The second part is that I would also appreciate it if you would put a freeze on recruiting and processing of any new hires for the same amount of time," says Herb. "I have already spoken to Captain Lewis, and he tells me that there are three classes currently in the academy training, and the recruiting people are ready to approve another four to start soon. I need a hold on all of that."

"How much time are you requiring, Herb?"

"At least four weeks."

"Four weeks!" says Wilson.

"Maybe five," Herb adds.

"You're gonna have to give me one hell of a reason to approve all of that, Herb."

"I'll give you the best reason. To take down the PCO."

"How the hell is closing the academy gonna do that?" says Wilson.

"I need the academy as the training ground for several handpicked officers. They are all gonna be trained in a crash course in special weapons and tactics, a.k.a. SWAT training. Once all of these officers have been certified, we will start in on the PCO's operations, but some of these officers, though experienced, need the refresher and the training, and the newer officers also need the training and the experience."

"So you gonna take down the PCO?" says Wilson.

"Yes, sir, I am," replies Herb.

"Sounds good to me. I'll call Captain Lewis and start the process," says Wilson.

"One more thing, sir. I would appreciate it if you let the cadets have their time off with pay. Don't want them to suffer because of this," says Herb.

"Of course. I'll take care of it. Just make sure that all of this is worth it and you take those bastards down for good and keep me posted."

"Yes, sir. Thank you, sir," Herb says as he leaves the office. *Shit that went a lot smoother than I thought it would, and I have all of the answers I came for,* thinks Herb.

Herb knows that the plan is solid and doable and that the only reason the mayor would oppose would be that he is also in the PCO's pocket. But that was not the case. Despite all his flaws, he had not been bought by the PCO, and to Herb, that just moved the mayor off of his shit list. This is a very big list that continues to grow, and at the top lies the heads of the PCO.

CHAPTER 14

Loyalty Is Everything

One of the first things the PCO decided to do when they started taking over the drug game in Philly was to move their money around. Of course they had investments in drugs and prostitution, but they also had quite a few legitimate businesses as well, one of these legitimate businesses being a meat-packing plant in South Philly. It was owned by some old mafia boss's nephew who signed over the plant to the PCO and mysteriously disappeared. It had some hard-to-pronounce Italian name, so everyone just called it the Plant. Despite appearances, the Plant did good business and had multimillion-dollar contracts with several of the major dog food companies as a supplier of various meats and meat parts. The PCO made good profit off the Plant with little overhead. And their money was divided into various accounts in various banks in and out of Philly. The whole processes was so efficiently run that this was one of the few businesses they owned where they didn't have to make monthly visits in order to collect their cash and see to the affairs of business personally.

So whenever a member of the PCO came to the Plant, it was to handle a different kind of business. The Plant was another of their various locations where they conducted their interrogations. This was Rock's favorite place to interrogate niggas, because after twenty or thirty minutes butt-ass naked in one of the Plant's freezers hanging from a meat hook, most niggas would tell you anything you wanted to know.

That being said, D and Rock couldn't help but be a little curious as to why K-Block wanted to meet them here at midnight. Both Rock and D pull up to the Plant at the same time, each driving one of the PCO's signature black Beemers.

"Yo, what the fuck is this all about?" Rock says to D as they enter the building.

"Fuck if I know, nigga, but if Block called us here, you know it's for a damn good reason," replies D.

They continue walking through the city-block-long plant, and they enter the executive office area and head to the main office where K-Block was waiting for them.

"'Sup, my niggas," Block greets them as they walk through the office door.

"Yo, K-Block. What's this all about?" asks D.

"Right. Straight to the point, D. I've always liked that about you," says Block. "I brought you both here to tell you something."

"So what is it?" asks D.

"Simply put, I love you niggas. You my fucking family, but above all that, I'm loyal to you niggas above all others," says Block.

"I feel you, nigga!" says Rock. "But I know you didn't call us the fuck out here just for that shit!"

"See, Rock, you family, and if you was any other nigga, I would have shot you dead right now for not taking what I just said in the serious manner that I meant it," says Block.

"Fuck you mean, Block? I take it serious and shit, but that shit you could have said over the phone or sent a letter or text. We damn sure didn't have to come all the way out here to hear it, feel me?" says Rock.

"I feel you, nigga, but you ain't feeling me!" says Block.

Sensing the tension rising in the room, D speaks. "Yo, Block, you know we love you too, my nigga, but why we have to come out here to hear it?"

"Why?" asks Block. "Because you niggas needed not only to hear what I was saying, but you needed to feel what I was saying too, and no fucking letter or text would cover it. The both of you missed my point entirely. The key words are *love, family*, and *loyalty*. *Loyalty*, niggas. Feel me?"

"Cool, nigga, we feel you. But—"

D is cut off by Block. "Follow me, niggas," says Block.

They leave the office, head down the stairs to the plant area, and walk the few minutes it takes to get to the last freezer in the back of the plant. When they get there, they are greeted by about six niggas standing outside the door. As they approach, one opens the door to the massive freezer to let them in. Inside, they see the young bull Low and two other niggas beating the shit out of a piece of meat hanging in the middle of the freezer like on some ol' *Rocky*-type shit. When they move in a little closer, D and Rock see that the piece of meat that Low and the niggas are beating up isn't a piece of meat at all but the nigga Dirty.

"Yo, Block what's this about, man?" says D. "Like I was saying to you niggas earlier, I love you and am loyal to you niggas above all others. And do you know why? It's because I know you are loyal to me above all others. We family. Our loyalty is unquestioned! And this . . . this nigga, this piece of shit dares to question our loyalty to one another. This muthafucka dares to try and put us against one another. So with that being said, you got something you want to tell me, D?"

"What the fuck are you talkin' about, Block? I don't have shi—" D pauses and thinks back to the last time he was around that nigga Dirty and remembers the phone conversation. "Oh shit. Yeah, my nigga Shan called me a couple of days ago and wants a meet wit' ya."

"Why you just now tellin me, D?" Block replies.

"Look, nigga, I told her I would set it up, but I started to have second thoughts about it. I was starting to lean toward not doing it at all. Is that what this is all about? You mean to tell me this bitch-ass nigga came running to you about this?" D says, now staring straight at that muthafucka Dirty.

"Yeah, my nigga," says Block. "This faggot-ass nigga actually thought he was gonna earn some kind of brownie points with me by snitchin' you out, talkin' shit like you trying to set me up. Plottin' to take me out wit' Shan an' shit."

D walks over to Dirty's battered and bloody body and gives him two swift shots to the body and one stiff one to the head, knocking out another one of Dirty's teeth. Low and the boys have been working over this nigga for the better part of the day, and he lost at least three teeth already in the process.

"This nigga won't miss one more," says Low.

D looks at Low and says, "I thought this nigga was ya man?"

"Fuck all that noise?" replies Low. "This nigga just work the block wit' me. PCO is the only thing I'm loyal to."

D cracks a grin. "I feel you, my nigga. That's what the fuck I'm talkin' about." D then looks at Block.

"Yo, my nigga, you know I didn't mean no disrespect. I just know how all you feel about that Shan situation. I figured I would just let sleeping dogs lie, know what I mean?"

"Yeah, my nigga, I feel you. At first, I was just gonna tell you 'Fuck that bitch,' but now . . . Go ahead. Set the shit up." Block heads for the door. "And by the way, that nigga on the meat hook is my gift to you."

"My nigga," says D as he pulls his nine and takes sight on that hanging nigga. "Good night, muthafucka."

CHAPTER 15

Training Day

"Okay, you maggots! Move, move, move!" screams drill instructor Taylor. *"Nobody quits, and nobody leaves until you all finish this course in under four minutes and thirty secs. Is that clear?"*

"Yes, sir!" scream the officers.

Drill instructor Taylor, twenty-five-year veteran of the PPD, SWAT trainer and team commander. One of the twenty officers handpicked by Commissioner Jackson for his special task force whose sole purpose is to take down the PCO.

"How are they holding up, Drill?" asks Herb.

"So far, so good, Commissioner. We still have a long way to go though. The upside is that all the officers are willing and giving one hundred percent effort—even the ones with no prior SWAT training. Even the most senior veteran officers are falling in line, which is surprising."

"It's no surprise really, Drill. Every one of them knows what's at stake and failure is not an option. I would expect no less than one hundred percent from each and every one of them," says Herb. "Call them in, Drill."

"Yes, sir," replies DI Taylor. *"All right, you maggots, front and center!"* shouts Taylor as he blows his whistle.

All the officers move to the position of Taylor and the commissioner with haste and fall in a platoon formation, each officer standing at attention.

"At ease," says Herb. "This is day 1. Numero uno. The beginning. I say that like it's the first day of your lives, because it is. Each of you was picked for this task force by me for a variety of reasons. First and foremost, you are all honest, good, uncorrupted police officers. And as ashamed as I am to say this, you are the minority. The unfortunate truth is that the Philadelphia Police Department has become corrupt, decadent, unscrupulous, untrustworthy, venal, and downright dishonorable.

"And at the top of all this decay is the PCO. Never in the history of this city has there been any one group of thugs and killers like this. They have managed to get a stranglehold on ninety percent of this city's crime in under eight months through torture and an unprecedented amount of bloodshed and bribes to top city officials.

"Well, I'm here to tell you today, on this training day, that when you are ready, I will put you in harm's way. I will ask of you what none has asked of you before. To be the shield and sword of this city. To protect the innocent and strike down any and all who corrupt the badge and this city. I will ask you to be prepared to be loved and hated at the same time. Your love will come from the innocent we have vowed to protect. But your hate among others will come from the people who once loved you, the corrupted men and women of the force. They will turn on you, and that's a fact. You will no longer belong to the frat—the brotherhood, if you will—that binds all officers of the law. You will not belong because through our actions, we will bring to light their corruption.

"But know this: we are fighting the good fight, we are on the right side, and we will not stop till the PPD is wiped clean of all PCO influence and we have eradicated the PCO once and for all. This is what I expect, and nothing less. If any of you feel that this is too much, then you should not return to this place tomorrow."

Without another word, Herb turns and leaves the training academy.

DI Taylor continues with the training they all came here to do. By the end of the day, all the officers are tired and beat but not broken, and at 6:30 a.m. the next morning, they have all returned.

Chapter 16

Bitches—Can't Live with 'Em . . .

"This is so wrong. This is so wrong, Rock."

"I know girl, but I won't tell if you won't."

"But, mmmmm, this is so fuckin' wrong. What if he finds out?"

"He won't, girl. Just relax."

"Mmmmm. Oh my . . . *Shit*, I'm coming again. *Sssssssshhhhiiiiittttt!*"

"That's what I'm talking about, girl. I knew you liked me. Shit, girl, I gotta hit that one more time before we leave."

"Fuck, Rock, don't you ever get enough? Shit, I already came four times, and I gotta get home before he gets back."

"Shit, one more time ain't gonna hurt, girl. Open them fuckin' legs back up and let me in."

"Shit, shit, *sssshhhhhiiiittttt!* Fuck, this dick is so fuckin' good. It must run in the family."

And in another part of the city...

"So what the fuck did you wanna see me for?"

"I missed you!"

"Ha!"

"I wanna come home. I want us to be a family again."

"Bitch, are you out of your fuckin' mind?"

"No, I just still love you and always have and always will."

"Love me? Love me? Did you love me when you were fuckin' that other nigga, *huh*? Did you fuckin' love me when you displayed to the city how you were fuckin' playin' me, or was you lovin' me when you was sneakin' and creepin' and laughing at me with your ho-ass sister? Was you fuckin' lovin' me then, Shan?"

"Kelly, listen!"

"No, bitch, you listen. Kelly is dead. The Kelly you knew anyway. He died that night, and this muthafucka you see before you now was born. I own this fuckin' city now and every fucking thing and body in it, so I can't help but think that maybe you wanna come back now because I gots shit on smash now."

"Kelly, it's not like that!"

"The fuck if it ain't. You know what hurt me the most about that night? Not the fact that you have been playing me all along, even though that shit hurt like hell. But the fact you never, ever gave a shit about me in the first place—that you were just using me until the next big thing smoking came along. I was just someone to take care of you and the kids, a fuckin' live-in babysitter, a fuckin' sucker."

"Kelly, please listen to me. It was never like that. Baby, I'm sorry. I made a big—a fuckin' huge mistake. Baby, please understand. I was confused and scared."

"Confused! Scared! About what, Shan? What the fuck was so confusing and scary that you would do that to me, huh? *What?*"

"Baby, please listen and remember. We was going through a rough patch in our marriage and financially, and I was scared for our future, for the kids' future. I didn't know how you would react to knowing the truth about them, and I was scared and wanted to tell you every day that they weren't your kids. But—"

"But what? You was having too much fun playing me?"

"I was afraid you wouldn't love them no more, you wouldn't love me no more. I'm sorry, but it was too much to bear. And after living with it for so long, I just could never bring myself to tell you."

"Woman, even now I can't blame them kids for your mistakes. Although I'm not much of a father these days, them kids are well taken care of. But I know you know that already."

"I do. I also know that they miss you ver—!"

"You can stop right there, bitch! I hoped you had something more in mind when you came in here than to try and have me reminisce on old times when we was a happy family and shit. Trying to make me feel all guilty and shit 'cause I can't be there for them kids. Because I hope you remember the last time we spoke. I hope you remember what I said to you. Make no mistake, I meant every word. The only reason you are standing here now is that D is the one who approached me and asked for you. Otherwise, you and your slut-ass sister would be dead by now. So unless you have something better to say, I advise you to get the fuck out of here. Besides, it's time for my eight o'clock appointment."

And almost on cue with K-Block's words, two fine-ass freaks walk through the door. Almost immediately, one starts tongue-kissing him while the other undoes his belt and pulls down his pants and starts sucking the shit out of his dick. Soon after, the other freak starts to assist the girl in sucking his dick and balls.

All the while, Shan looks on in astonishment.

K-Block looks up and is pleased with the reaction from Shan. "You still here, bitch? You want to join in? Get the fuck on before I have you on your knees too."

Shan, now wide-eyed and disgusted at the thought, runs out of the office and out of the house, tears starting to run from her eyes.

Back inside, the two freaks continue sucking on K-Block's dick and balls, and when he busts, he lets them both take it in the face, and they love it.

"All right, go on to the room. I'll be there in a minute. Feel free to start without me."

Without saying a word, they both get off their knees and head to the room as instructed, and along the way, they start kissing and fondling each other.

When they leave, K-Block pulls out his cell and calls D. "Sup, nigga? Where you at?"

"Headed to the crib right now. Gonna fuck the shit outta Tracy, and then I'll see you at the Pic around eleven o'clock." replies D.

"Cool, nigga. That will give me time to fuck these two bitches real good," says Block.

"Yo, how did that shit go with Shan?" asks D.

"It went like I thought it would, my nigga. I'll see you at the Pic. Peace!"

"Peace, nigga!"

They hang up.

Now, thinks Block as he heads into the room where the two freaks are waiting for him, *on to more important things!*

And as suggested, they started without him. When he enters the room, they are in a sixty-nine position, eating the shit out of each other's pussies.

When Block enters the room and sees this, his dick gets immediately hard, and he couldn't get his clothes off fast enough to join in. And join in he does.

Block loved women and he had a lot of control, but every now and then, he would indulge himself like this. As soon as he approaches the bed, the two freaks stop what they are doing and start to focus on him.

Diamond, the smaller of the two freaks, go for Block's dick like a pit bull at some raw meat. She grabs it as soon as he comes near and starts sucking vigorously, massaging his balls at the same time. Up and down, she goes to work on his long, hard, thick shaft while Torques, the thicker of the two, starts to tongue-kiss him down.

Block grabs Torques by the waist—her legs open almost instinctively— puts her on his shoulders so that her pussy is right in his face, and he goes to work, sucking and slurping on her clit, his tongue in and out her pussy. Torques could not contain her moans and screams of pleasure, which only turn on Diamond more as she starts to suck Block's dick harder and faster, wanting him to cum in her mouth so bad. Diamond then turns around, her hand still gripping his hard member, and sticks it in her now dripping pussy and starts to work that ass back and forth, round and round, while at the same time, without missing a beat, still with Torques on his shoulders and her dripping pussy in his face, he starts to stroke Diamond's hot, wet pussy, pounding slowly at first then faster. Now both Diamond and Torques are moaning and screaming with pleasure. After several minutes of this, Block puts Torques down and pulls his still hard dick out of Diamond.

He motions for them to trade places. Now he is pounding Torques's hot, throbbing pussy with Diamond on his shoulders and in his mouth. The freaks continue their moans of ecstasy.

Once finished with that position, the freaks motion for Block to lie down. Diamond jumps back on his dick, and Torques has her pussy back in his face. Soon they are going back and forth, multiple positions. By this time, the freaks have each cum about seven or eight times apiece. Then when it's time for Block to bust, they both take it in the face, licking and sucking out every last drop. They are all exhausted.

"Tracy, I'm home, girl! Where you at? Got some good hard dick for you. Hey, girl, you hear me?" yells out D. *Where the fuck this bitch at?* D thinks.

"Damn!, girl, this pussy is so fuckin' good. Oh shit, I'm cummin' again!"

"Damn!, Rock, that was some fuckin' good dick. Got my legs all shakin' an' shit. What time is it?"

"A little after nine forty-five."

"*Shit, Rock! D gonna be home any minute.* You gotta get me home fast. *Shit,* I knew this was a fuckin' mistake. I knew it," says Tracy as she hurries to put her clothes back on and climb into the front seat to try to make herself look as if she wasn't having sex for the past hour and a half in the backseat of a car.

"Calm down, ma. I got ya covered. I'll just tell him you was with me. We got bored waiting on him, so we went to the bar for a drink," says Rock with confidence.

"Are you the fuck crazy, Rock? You can't tell D no shit like that! He know I can't stand your black ass and I wouldn't go nowhere with you. You tell him that shit, and he gonna know something's up for sure," says Tracy.

"And so the fuck what? If he did know, ain't like the nigga can beat my ass. Anyway, you know, I'm sure he would rather it be me than some lame-ass nigga. You know, keeping it all in the family an' shit," Rock says with a smile.

Tracy looks at Rock as if he's crazy. "Nigga, don't get this shit twisted. I love my boo. This here was just a fuck, nothing more. And it ain't never gonna happen again."

"Whatever, bitch. You said that shit the last time. And the time before that. Oh, and the time before that, and so on. Need I go on?"

"Whatever, nigga. Just get me the fuck home and keep your mouth closed about this shit. *Shit,* he called my phone. Change of plan, don't take me home. Gotta make a detour."

Twenty minutes later, Tracy comes through the door with her girlfriend Dez, and there to greet them is a now heated D.

"Bitch, where the fuck you been?" says a very pissed-off D.

"Calm down, sweetie. I was just out with Dez. I got bored waiting for you to come home, so we went to the bar for a drink."

"So why the fuck didn't you answer your phone then?" says D.

"Baby, you know how loud that music be in there an' shit. I didn't hear it," responds Tracy. "Why you so fuckin' hyped? What, a bitch can't go out for a drink no more?"

"Look, if you gonna be somewhere loud, then put your cell on vibrate like I told you before. I gotta be able to contact you at all times. You know these niggas is grimy out there. They might try and get to me through you, dig me?"

"I dig you, baby. Don't worry. You know I keeps my strap on me always. I'm good, baby. But it's nice to see you still worry about me, booboo."

"Well, you know . . . Anyway, I'm headed out for a while. See ya later, babe."

"All right, baby. Be safe. I'll see you when you get home."

And as soon as the door closes, Dez says, "Giiirrrrlllll, oh my god, that was close!"

"Shit, girl. Who you tellin'? I'm so glad I caught you at home tonight. I needed to get myself together before coming here, and he needed to see me walk in with you for him to believe that bullshit I just fed him," says Tracy.

"Girl, damn, you stay fucking with some thug-ass niggas. But at least you got you a PCO nigga, so why the fuck you cheating? He not fucking you good no more? Because you used to always brag on D's dick. And better yet, who you cheating with? Them PCO niggas is at the top of the food chain right now out in them streets, so I know whoever you fuckin' with ain't getting that money like D."

"Best you don't know everything I do, girlfriend. Just know D is my boo, and I plan on keeping it like that."

"Anyway, Tracy, fuck all ya secrets. What's up with D's brother, Block? I hear he ain't got nobody, and I would fit in real nice as the first lady of the PCO, ya heard?"

"I hear ya, bitch, but Kelly is someone I wouldn't hook my worst enemy up with, so you are out of the question."

"Awww, but why? He's so cute. And he gots paper stacked to the ceiling," says Dez.

"Because, girl, frankly, he scares the shit out of me."

CHAPTER 17

Here We Go

"Officers, you made it! This is the last day of training. It's been a long and hard five weeks, but you all made it, and tomorrow, we go to work. Just know this: I am proud of each and every one of you. You have thus far exceeded my expectations. Now, as I promised you 5 weeks ago, it's time for me to put you in harm's way. So tonight, go home, spend time with your wives and husbands. Kiss and hold your children a little bit longer tonight because tomorrow, it's time to shake things up. Tomorrow, it's time to raise some hell with the PCO," says an excited Herb.

"Tomorrow, nigga! Tomorrow we gonna do it all over again. Make this money, fuck these fine-ass, freak-ass bitches, and get high as fucking kites," says D.

"Yeah, my nigga, I feel you," replies Rock. "Yo, D, where the fuck is Block, my nigga? We been here like an hour already, and that nigga still not here."

Just then K-Block steps through the door and takes a seat in the booth.

"Yo, my nigga, we was starting to get worried. You ain't never the last one to show up when we hang out," says Rock.

"Yeah, my nigga, I was about to call you if you didn't show by the time I finished this beer," says D.

"Yo, my niggas, you know I was putting my thing down with those two freaks Diamond and Torques," replies Block.

"Shit those two fuckin' freaks gave me a real workout. I straight clocked out for about twenty minutes after fuckin' wit' them."

"I feel you, my nigga, I feel you. I was fucking this real freak-ass bitch today too. That pussy was good as a muthafucka. Almost put my ass to sleep," says Rock with a grin.

"Shit, I went home, my bitch wasn't even the fuck there. Out drinking with her tramp-ass girlfriend and shit, so I ain't get no fucking pussy before comin' in here. So you know I'm pullin' something out of here tonight!" says D.

"I'll drink to that, my nigga" says Block.

Damn, this nigga never late, and he late tonight of all nights. This could not be more perfect if I planned this shit, Rock thinks and smiles as he takes a drink from his beer. *Could not be more fuckin' perfect.*

Five a.m. the next day, in the squad room of the Thirty-First Precinct, currently the headquarters of the task force for what is to become known as Operation Takedown, the twenty handpicked, specially trained officers report for a roll call and morning briefing, addressed by Commissioner Jackson.

"Okay, let's get down to business. Here is what we know. From the outside, it seems that the PCO is run by three individuals, starting on the left"—the commissioner points to one of three pictures hanging on a presentation easel—"we have Rashawn Franklin Karr, a.k.a. Rock. Our file on this guy seems to go on forever. Needless to say, a career criminal. This guy has seen and done it all. Everything from breaking and entering, minor to major drug busts, to rape and murder charges. I say *charges* because he was never convicted on any of the rapes or murders because in every case, the star witnesses or the victims mysteriously disappear. This guy is a train' wreck waiting to happen. He has been incarcerated multiple times and has a documented explosive temper.

"On the right, we have Devon Lewis Karr, a.k.a. D. He is the younger of the two Karr boys and what you might call Rock Light. His criminal records don't go past his juvenile years, although he also has a very well-known volatile temper. No rapes or murders in his jacket but plenty of breaking and entering, home invasions, and carjacking. All of that, ladies and gentlemen, between the ages of twelve and fifteen. Then, all of a sudden, it stops, and we believe we know why. Both Rock and D come from the same broken home. Father was a drunk who left them very young under the care of their crack-addict mother, et cetera, et cetera. But at the age of sixteen, D went to live with his older half sister who, at the time, was married to our last man, Kelly Treshawn Brown. And this is where it starts to get real interesting.

"Kelly Treshawn Brown, a.k.a. K-Block, a.k.a. Block, has no police record. Nothing, zero, zip, zilch."

If they weren't listening before, they are now, because the look of amazement and puzzlement on the faces of every officer in the room is noticed by the commissioner.

"I'm glad to see I have your attention. And yes, you heard me right. K-Block has no criminal record. Nothing—not a speeding ticket, parking violation. Nothing. And we believe he is possibly the most dangerous of the three. Now when I started this briefing, I said that from the outside, it seems that the PCO is run by all three of these men. But our intelligence believes that K-Block is the boss of the PCO, followed closely by D and then the muscle Rock. That is what we believe, but we can't be sure. Intelligence on the PCO is very scarce, but we need to know the command structure of the PCO before we can attack it and bring it down. So that being said, our first order of business will be intelligence gathering, but in order to get any info on the PCO, we're going to have to rattle their cages a little and see what falls out."

And rattle their cages they did. Over the next three months, Operation Takedown is up and running at full force. The Task Force needed intel, and intel they got. They hit hard and shook down all known PCO drug houses and illegitimate businesses. They interrogated and locked up multiple dealers, buyers, and the like. With the intel they gathered, they are able to shake down some of the PCO's less-known businesses as well. They also launch a media campaign against the PCO with the assistance of the mayor.

The identity of every member of the Task Force is kept top secret. Every shakedown, every hit on the PCO, they wear masks and no name tags and no badges. Also, every officer outside of the Task Force is reassigned out of the Thirty-First Precinct.

The building becomes the Task Force's headquarters. No one outside of the task force officers is allowed to enter the building. To the general public, this building is especially off-limits. All complaints and reports of crime and the like are diverted to the Twenty-Ninth Precinct.

The operation is starting to see a little success with their efforts, but they need more. They still couldn't get close enough to the heads of the PCO to do any real damage. Even with the drug houses and businesses they take down, it doesn't take long for the PCO to set up shop in another location, and it is business as usual. The turnaround sometimes takes less than an hour. They have to do something to get at the heads of the PCO. Commissioner Jackson has a radical thought.

A press conference is called, and with the mayor by his side, Commissioner Jackson releases this statement: "Ladies and gentlemen of the press, for far too long this city has been plagued by a cancer. A cancer that has struck fear into the hearts of good, honest, hardworking citizens. This cancer runs our streets with fear and corruption, using money, power, and influence at a street level and a political level to taint even the most sacred of this city's institutions, giving its citizens nowhere to turn for help. This cancer has even managed to touch my life in a very personal way.

"But the good news is, this cancer has been identified. This cancer has a name: the PCO. Through the hard work and dedication of members of what is simply known as the Task Force, which is comprised of several honest, uncorrupted, specially trained police officers, we, with support and the assistance of the mayor's office, have initiated Operation Takedown, a campaign to rid this city of its cancer, the PCO."

Immediately, the press tries to ask multiple questions, which they are told to hold.

Commissioner Jackson continues. "Since the start of Operation Takedown, we have had some strides closing down drug houses and businesses in various neighborhoods. But the job is far from over. We have, also through our investigation, discovered the heads of the PCO: Rashawn Franklin Karr and his brother, Devon Lewis Karr, two petty career criminals, and Kelly Treshawn Brown, an unknown, a nobody with delusions of grandeur.

"These, my fellow citizens, are the caliber of men who hold this city hostage with nothing more than smoke and mirrors. Their power is an illusion. These men are nothing more than cowards who use guns and violence to bully the weak and defenseless. I say to you—no, I swear to you now—this reign of terror will end and all involved, especially these cowards, will be brought to justice. The buck stops here. Thank you."

As Commissioner Jackson leaves the podium, he is bombarded with questions, to which he replies, "No comment."

"Do you believe this shit? Has that muthafucka lost his fuckin' mind?" Rock asks.

"Yo, D, get some of the boys and strap up. We gonna deal wit' this nigga once and for all," says Rock.

"Yo, I definitely feel you on that. We gotta remind this muthafucka who he dealing with," says D.

"Yo, Block, you ridin' or what?" asks D.

"No," says Block.

"No? What the fuck you mean *no*? You heard that punk-ass Commissioner call us the fuck out. We gotta ride, nigga. The streets is watchin," says Rock.

"You heard me, muthafucka. I said *no*. I ain't going nowhere, and neither are you two," says Block.

"*Fuck* you mean, nigga? You don't—"

But before Rock could finish his sentence, Block is on him, gets him gripped up and slammed against the wall. Both Rock and D are surprised. They know Block got mad fight game but don't really know how strong he is. Size-wise Rock was the biggest of the three of them and all muscle and outweighed Block by about fifty pounds. Just looking at them, no one would have thought Block could manhandle Rock like this.

"You listen to me, and you listen good. The decisions and the moves we make ain't got shit to do with what the streets is looking at. Get you fuckin' head out of your fuckin' ass. That muthafucka is baitin' us, setting a trap, and your dumb muthafuckin' ass can't wait to run in and spring it."

"Yo, what you mean, Block?" D interjects.

Block releases his grip on Rock and explains. "This muthafucka and his so-called Task Force have been running around the city for the past three months, shaking down our smaller drug fronts and businesses, trying to get at us, but they ain't putting no kind of dent in business, and they know it. If they had anything on us at all, they would have run up in here with the National Guard trying to arrest us, but they haven't. Why? 'Cause they ain't got shit. So now what do they do? They now start talking all kinds of reckless shit on the news, trying to get us all riled up so we can run out on some ol' 'The streets are watchin'' bullshit, do some dumb shit like y'all was about to do, and get arrested. I told y'all niggas, we gotta be MOB at all times, and MOB ain't just 'money over bitches.' It also means 'money over bullshit.' We run this fuckin' city, and everybody knows it. We are above this petty street-level shit. Now you niggas gotta start looking at the big fuckin' picture. This ain't about no 'Aww, this nigga disrespected me. Now I gotta show out for the streets' type shit. Niggas, we own the streets and ain't gotta show or prove a muthafuckin' thing. That top-cop nigga gotta come harder than that."

"I feel you block. No doubt," says D.

Rock says nothing, but both Block and D see that he is still seething and may still do something stupid.

"Yo, nobody makes no moves on this nigga nobody. Pass the word to the crew and all the workers too, in case anybody gets any bright ideals. Nobody is to move on this nigga or his fam. Not yet, anyway."

CHAPTER 18

Trust

It's been almost a year since PCO took over the streets of Philadelphia.

The nigga Low done worked his way up the ladder, proving his loyalty time after time. Low is now a high-ranking lieutenant in the PCO organization. Low started just hustling weed and rock on the corners, then he moved up to muscle and doing hits for the PCO. Block noticed this little nigga from the beginning and after a while made him a lieutenant, putting him in charge of the businesses (legit and nonlegit) in South Philly. Low ran that shit too. He only answered to Block, D, or Rock, and everyone knew it and couldn't tell him shit. And he didn't take any either. This cocky now eighteen-year-old nigga knew his business, and even the old G's couldn't get shit past him.

In fact, it was Low who found out how Raz's crew was still doing business. They were passing out pagers and throwaway cell phones to all their customers and changed the location of where they were dealing every day.

When he told Rock, they moved on them niggas and locked down the rest of South Philly. Of course, Rock had taken all the credit. Low didn't care though. He was a loyal PCO soldier through and through. They were like his family, and as far as he was concerned, when the PCO was doing good, he was doing good.

Three days after the police commissioner's press conference, it is business as usual, or so it seems. It looks like Rock has calmed down some, and things appear to be all good. Block is headed out of town, and so is D. They get together with Rock and Low in the office to discuss the details of their individual trips.

Block is headed to Cuba on a private plane to meet up with his connect Pablo to discuss setting up a new deal that would provide more product for the PCO at a lower cost, as well as some other shit.

D is heading out to making the rounds from Delaware to New Jersey and then New York. It is time to expand the PCO's businesses, and they had been slowly moving into various territories in each of these states, and D is going to check on progress, particularly in New York. PCO wants to hit the Big Apple hard and fast, just like they did Philly, and take over the drug game as quickly and smoothly as possible. They anticipate little trouble from the drug gangs and the like but know they would have some serious issues with the Mafia. The main question at this point is, Do they negotiate with the mob, or just say fuck 'em and go to war? When they all get together again, they would decide based on D's intel of the areas. So for a week or two, that would leave Rock in charge of PCO's normal day-to-day businesses and Low would be his second in command.

Just as soon as Block and D leave town, Rock is knocking on Tracy's door, and five minutes after that, they are fuckin' like rabbits. Rock is lovin' this shit. All the money, all the power, and all the women. It is too much for him to give up. After bustin' his third nut, he picks up the phone and calls Low. "Yo, nigga, get me three or four niggas strapped up and ready to ride. We hittin' that fuckin' pig today."

"Didn't Block say wasn't nobody to move on this nigga or his fam?" replies Low.

"Look, muthafucka, what Block said or didn't say don't mean shit right now. I'm the HNIC, and don't fuckin' forget it," says Rock. "Get them niggas ready. I'll be at the spot in an hour."

An hour later, Rock pulls up and finds three niggas ready to ride, sitting in a beat-up brown Pontiac, ready to roll. "Yo, what y'all niggas doing?" yells Rock. "Get the fuck out of that piece of shit and get in! We rollin' on this muthafucka in style. We don't need to fuckin' hide who we are with stolen cars and ski masks and shit. I want them niggas to know just who the fuck hit 'em."

Low isn't with them but observes this scene from the front third-story office window of the house where most of their business was discussed. Low shakes his head slightly and thinks *This shit is gonna end bad.*

About 3:30 p.m., Rock pulls up to City Hall. As luck would have it, the mayor is leavin' for the day with the commissioner by his side. They seem oblivious to what is going on around them as they discuss who knows what. Neither of them notice the jet-black 745 with the tinted windows holding up this rush hour traffic roll down the windows.

CHAPTER 19

Time to Expand

After about ten days, D finished his business in Delaware and New Jersey, and business was good. The PCO had a very strong presence in both states. In fact, they practically had the whole of the Delaware drug game on smash, and New Jersey wasn't far behind. Camden and Trenton were already getting all their supply from the PCO exclusively, and it was just a matter of time till Jersey was on lock.

New York, however, was proving to be a bit difficult. The small-time drug gangs folded and assimilated into the PCO, but the Italian Mafia was proving to be a bit more difficult. D wasn't surprised though. They had planned for that. D was going to have a sitdown with the mob bosses and, depending on the outcome of that meeting, would decide the next move.

D knew that this meeting would be a difficult one for him. He knew that the Italians didn't respect the blacks no matter how much money or power they had. To them, he knew, he would never be anything more than a fuckin' nigga, a monkey, or a mullie as they liked to call us. D also knew his own temper, and one disrespectful word from one of these linguine-dick muthafuckas could set him the fuck off, and then it's all-out fucking war from the door. But D knew that Block was counting on him to handle this situation in a professional manner.

MOB over all. It's all about getting money. Nothing else gotta keep my temper in check, D keeps telling himself over and over. D knows that the only time Block would kill or authorize a kill against someone is if the PCO's paper is involved. Even the night he killed Raz, all the other bullshit aside, was all about the paper. *After Block killed that bitch-ass nigga, we moved in on all of his business fast and hard. Niggas on the streets didn't know what the fuck to do. Razmon out of the picture, and these three new niggas running the whole fucking thing now. No one would have ever saw this shit coming. Thanks to Block's planning and our execution of the plan, following his lead and shit, we fucking kings out here. Shit, normally Block would handle this negotiation shit 'cause he knows how I gets the fuck down and he really knows he can't send Rock out on no shit like this—we would be at war before we even started. He says I can handle it. He must really have faith in me. I'll try not to let him down, but I just don't know about this one.*

Ten minutes later, the car D is being driven in stops, interrupting his train of thought as the driver informs him that they have arrived. After the driver opens the rear passenger door, D steps out of the car and looks up at the sign: Giovanni's Italian Restaurant. He steps into the restaurant, escorted by his driver and another man from the front passager seat.

He was greeted at the door by underboss, Lugi Grazsi, and enforcer Jimmy "One Finger" Nucci.

"Gentlemen, welcome to our little establishment," says Grazsi.

"Very nice to be here," says D.

"Follow me," says Grazsi.

Grazsi leads them to the back of the restaurant, which is very crowded for twelve o'clock, and to the back past the kitchen, where chefs are busy cooking and preparing and bus boys are busy washing dishes and running in and out. They head toward the storage room and up a flight of stairs to what looks to be an apartment, but there is no furniture, only a table and chairs filled with some of New York's most notorious and most wanted mobsters. Among them was Antonio Bregetti, the boss of bosses or the newest and youngest-ever godfather of the New York crime families. He greets his guess with a smile, which is more than D expected. He also didn't expect to see Bregetti at this meet, but he was just going to roll with it and watch out for the setup.

After five days of negotiations, D returns from New York. As luck would have it, Block is returning from his trip the same day, a couple of hours after D. So D drives to the airport to pick him up. "'Sup, my nigga? How was your trip?" asks D.

"Good, real good. Gots some business to discuss when we get back to the office. The suppliers and I came to a very lucrative agreement. What about your trips?" asks Block.

"My brother, Delaware and New Jersey belong to us, hands down."

"What about New York? How's that looking?"

"You'll be surprised with what went down. I'll tell you and Rock all about it when we get to the office."

Chapter 20

Absent

Back in the office, D and Block start to discuss the events and outcomes of their individual trips. They call Rock and Low to come and join them. Low is in South Philly attending to PCO business when they call. Rock never answers his cell. D leaves him a message. When Low returns, he is greeted by D and Block. Block is sitting in his normal position behind the big wooden desk, and D is posted up on the corner of the desk on his cell. They start to fill him in on their trips.

D asks, "Where the hell is Rock? I done called that nigga five times. No answer."

Low responds, "I haven't seen him since the day you two left."

"What the fuck you mean you haven't seen him since we left? It's been over fuckin' two weeks," says D.

"It's just like I said, D. He bounced up outta here for a couple hours the day you left. He called me to get some niggas strapped up and ready, and an hour after that—"

"Strapped up and ready for what?" Block chimes in and starts to rise from his seat.

"He was gonna move on that Commissioner Jackson muthafucka," said Low.

"What the fuck you mean 'He was gonna move on Jackson'?" Block shouts. "What the fuck do *you mean*? After I told that muthafuc—" Block starts to calm himself, "Where is he?" asks Block.

Low replies, "I don't know where he is. I put the word out on the street and reached out to our informants in the PPD, and no one has seen or heard from him. Since that day, Jackson has been on the news, talking his normal bullshit, so I knew the hit never went down. And according to all of our sources, it's like he never even got close to Jackson at all. Nothing in the news or anything. It's like he just fell off the face of the earth."

"Fuck all that shit, Low," says D. "You get them niggas out there double time looking for my fuckin' brother, ya dig? You turn over every fuckin' rock, kick in every fuckin' door till you find him, got me?"

"Got you, D" says Low, and with that, he's out.

"*Fuck!*" shouts D. "What the fuck this nigga done got himself into, Block?"

"I don't know, D, but we have a bigger problem. You know what I'm sayin'."

"Yeah, I know, Block. What the fuck we gonna do with that nigga when we find him? He done crossed the fuckin' line and broke the rule."

The rule—loyalty to the PCO above all. The one rule that Block, D, and Rock had with each other. All decisions that they made, they followed without question, and Rock had broken this rule.

But he still my brother, D thinks as he walks into his home. *Tracy's out somewhere, probably spending my money, and the kids are in school.* D continues to think. *Good. Don't want to be around anyone right now anyway.* D heads to his lounge area to sit in his favorite most comfortable chair and nods off.

Shit, I should have seen this shit coming! That fuckin' Rock like a fuckin' pit bull. Can't let that nigga out of your sight for a second, Block thinks. *We gotta deal with this nigga, but shit, he still family. This can't end well.*

Block reaches for his cell and dials up Low. "You found him yet?" asks Block.

"Not yet," replies Low. "I've got every nigga on the streets with their eyes open, and I got a few niggas, including myself, watchin' his place and his usual hangouts. They all got instructions to contact me the second anyone sees him. I also got our informants in the PPD checking around all the districts as well. Don't worry. If he's in Philly anywhere, we'll find him."

And with that they hang up.

During this whole time that the PCO have been doing their thing, taking over the city, Block has never felt this anxious about anything. He knows according to their rule what had to be done to Rock—they all agreed on it when they started the PCO. Loyalty to the PCO above all, and the only punishment for breaking this rule is death, to be dealt by the other members of the PCO command structure, which of course, are D and himself. But how

Changes

could they kill their own brother? When they put the rule in place, it was more of an example to all other members of the PCO as to the depth of their loyalty to each other and an example of the loyalty that they expected from every member of the PCO from them on down. But they never thought in a million years that they would have to enforce it.

Also, Block knows that there are only two reasons that Rock would go against the rule. One, either his hotheadedness just got the best of him. Or two, he wanted to run the whole organization himself. The whole of the PCO under his command and his command only. Though he would never tell D, he always felt that it would come to this one day.

CHAPTER 21

The Day After

The morning of Raz's untimely, very gruesome death, D dropped Kelly off at his home. Upon his entry, he saw that his home was a mess. No doubt from Shan hurrying to get out before he came back. For a long time—what seemed like hours—Kelly just stood in the doorway, looking around, as if stuck in place. He stood there with a blank look on his face, just remembering. Remembering all the good times, all the laughs and all the lies and deceit. Before D dropped him off, Kelly told him to meet him back there by 4:00 a.m.

D pulled up right on time and also carrying Kelly's other request: about fifty gallons of gasoline in two twenty-five-gallon containers. They proceeded to pour the gas on every floor and piece of furniture in every room in the house. With the last two gallons, they made a trail from each room leading out the front door.

Kelly grabbed the one bag he packed and lit the fuse and watched as the flames followed the trail to each room. He then took one final look, closed the door, and turned and walked away to the car where D was waiting.

Kelly saw this as the most defining moment in his life. He felt reborn. He only took a few clothes and some old pictures of his kids and parents and let the rest burn. He made sure to put a little extra gasoline on any clothing that Shan left behind, just for good measure.

Driving away as the house started to burn, Kelly lit a Black&Mild and took a puff.

"So what's the plan?" asks D.

Kelly then goes through the wad of cash that he took off Raz after he killed him, which totaled about seven stacks. "Drop me off at the airport Hilton. Take these three Gs and take the plates off and dump then burn this car and pick up another one ASAP then head in. First things first, I'm gonna get me a good night's sleep, then we'll talk tomorrow."

Twenty minutes later, Kelly got out of the car and headed into the Hilton for a good night's sleep. And a good sleep was what he had. He knew that eventually the police would find Raz's burned-up, dismembered body in that old house down the Bottoms. And he knew that would eventually lead the police to his door because of all the people who saw him drive off with Raz in the trunk of his car. He burned anything and everything that could link him with Raz, even had D ditch and torch the car, so if the police ever caught up with him, he could say it was stolen, and no physical evidence would be recovered from the old house, his home, or his car. Knowing this, he would sleep good tonight—very, very good.

The next day, when he woke up, Kelly felt more refreshed and more focused than he had every felt before in his life. He sat up and called D. "'Sup, my nigga?"

"What's up?"

"You handle that piece of business for me yesterday?"

"Of course, my nigga. I dropped that car—"

"Not on the phone, my nigga. Never on the phone," Kelly quickly responded. "Yo, you and Rock just get yourselves together and get down here. I'm in room 512."

"All right, nigga, see you in a few," said D. "Later."

"Later."

After that phone conversation, Kelly called down and ordered some room service, jumped into the shower, and got ready for the events of the day. Ever since he woke up this morning, something seemed different. He felt different, he thought. He felt like he had a sense of purpose—something he never felt before. Sure, when he was with Shan and the kids, his whole purpose in life was to take care of them, but that always felt more like his duty than a purpose. When he woke up this morning, it was if everything was clear to him for the first time. He knew his purpose was to rise to the top by any means necessary, to take over Philly, to become the richest, most powerful nigga around, and to destroy anyone or anything that dared to try to stand in his way.

Kelly was a thinking man. Yeah, he could squabble with the best of them. But the muscle hustle wasn't his game. But he knew it was gonna take a lot of muscle as well as planning to get where he wanted to go and that was straight to the top.

Around about 12:00 p.m., D and Rock show up, and Kelly starts to lay it out for them. "Well, here it is, my niggas, the day and the time has come for us to take over this muthafuckin' city."

"That's what the fuck I'm talking about!" said D.

"Sounds real good my, nigga, but how the fuck we supposed to do it?" said Rock.

"I'm glad you fuckin' asked, Rock, because in order for this shit to work, we gonna have to work together in all things. We gonna have to go beyond family and work as one, but we all have a part to play.

"Rock, out of all of us, you have the most connections out in them streets, and in a minute, that's gonna mean a lot, because we need a lot of soldiers, and we need them fast.

"The streets are wide open now that Raz is out of the picture. We all know that there ain't one nigga in his organization that can step in and fill his shoes, so it's gonna be a lot of little niggas trying to go for the top spot. Fighting and confusion is gonna set in 'cause can't no little nigga ever fill a big nigga's shoes, and that's where we come in.

"First things first, we gotta take over Razmon's businesses, and we have to do it quick fast, and the only way that we can do it is we're gonna have to shed some blood, and a lot of it starting today. Rock, we gonna need you to round up ten of the hardest and hungriest shooter-type niggas. We gonna ride starting tonight.

"D, get Tracy and the kids to stay with her sister in Jersey for a while. Can't have no distractions and no niggas getting any bright ideas about getting at us through our families. You gotta do the same, Rock. Get your BM and kids out of the city for a while. My kids are already in New York with Shan's mom. All we need to worry about from now on is each other. If you niggas is down, we have got to have complete trust and loyalty to one another. Death before dishonor, muthafuckas."

And with that, Block pulled out one of his twin Glocks, dropped the clip, and pushed out three bullets. He then pulled out his knife, and on the casing of each bullet, he carved their initials. On one bullet, he put a *K*. On the second, he put a *D*. And on the third, he put an *R*. He set each one down on the table they had been sitting at and said, "Death before dishonor, and loyalty to each other above all. We each will take one of these bullets, but not the one with our initial on it, and we will keep it aside. If any one of us ever betrays this union that we have put together today, then it will be up to the other two to take that bullet and to put him the fuck down. Now if you down with this, pick up a bullet."

Block intentionally picked up the one with the R on it as Rock and D grabbed the other two. They held the bullets up for a moment, as if they were going to drink from them in this sort of dark communion. And so was born the Paper Chaser Organization.

And so it began. Not forty-eight hours after Block killed Razmon, the PCO started their initiative to take over Philly. Before the streets got too hot, Block, D, and Rock hit Razmon's home located just outside of Philadelphia County in Broomall. Razmon had a beautiful eight-bedroom home in a very secluded housing area on Route 309. Block took the liberty of not only relieving Raz of his money, but also taking his ID with address and his keys. Razmon's home was beautiful, nothing at all like what any of them expected. They were all expecting something out of *Scarface*—really gaudy- and tacky-like, but this was more like something off *Cribs* or *Lifestyles of the Rich and Famous*.

He had what you'd expect any black man to have: flat-screens, leather furniture, cable, PlayStations and Xbox's in every room. But it was real tasteful—something none of them were looking for.

But what they were looking for, they found: dates and times, contacts, financial info—everything they would need to start to take over Raz's business. Mostly what they found was info on his legal businesses. It seems Raz was too smart to keep too much info on his illegal shit in his home. That didn't worry them too much though. They had enough info on his street businesses to get their foot in the door, because the streets not only was watching but it stayed talking. And with this new info on his other businesses, they would take over his whole operation in no time.

Before he was laid off, Block was the network system administrator for a pharmaceutical company. His vast computer knowledge paid off here, because most of Razmon's financial info was on password-protected computers and backups. Block was able to hack these with little effort, and now with the keys to Raz's kingdom, there was no stopping them. They also managed to find his safe. Since none of them were professional safecrackers, Rock suggested blowing it up. Fortunately, among other things, Block found the combination to the safe in some computer files. Apparently, this was the cash Raz kept on hand for his legitimate business—a cool three million once it was all counted. And just like that, they all became millionaires.

Now that they had some cash and about ten "'bout it, 'bout it" niggas. Rock hit up one of his contacts, and two hours and twenty thousand later, they had the guns. Now was the time to let these niggas know just who the fuck they were.

They hit some of the most highly trafficked drug corners in North and South Philly. "PCO, muthafucka!" was heard all though the hoods, then came the shots. Multiple gunshots rang out, and a bunch of bodies hit the pavement. Eventually, they would recruit some of these corner-type niggas but right now, it was all about letting niggas know who they were and what they were about. They hit these niggas hard and fast, took all they cash and everything from the stash spots. In and out, quick and fast, before anyone knew what was happening. Bodies were dropping for days, and the cops were at a loss.

Block knew that although the body count was stacking up, they didn't have too much to fear from the cops. They weren't gonna move too fast or waste so much manpower on the murders of a few drug dealers, and anyway, all this shooting and killing wasn't nothing new to these neighborhoods. That's one of the reasons Block picked them. They could stack paper and product and really didn't have to worry about the cops too much.

Yeah, Block thought. *It's all going according to plan. Soon we will have all of Raz's businesses making money for us and all of his workers on the payroll. Those we let live, that is. Shouldn't be too hard to turn the average street earner to our way of thinking. But everybody else who had any kind of position of power in Raz's organization has got to go. Can't let them niggas live.*

K-Block was right. Within a month and a half, they had turned the streets of Philadelphia into a bloody graveyard, and they had succeeded in taking over at least 90 percent of Raz's organization.

Within two months, they started making more money and putting more product on the streets than Raz ever had by increasing their buying and putting more workers on the streets in different areas. For example, Raz never took his businesses outside of North and South Philly. PCO started moving in on the southwest and northeast parts of Philly. At first, being a predominately white area of Philadelphia, the northeast was normally off-limits to the average street hustler standing around on the corners. They would get booked before they could even set up shop.

The PCO got around this obstacle by recruiting some of the locals from the high schools and grade schools who thought that the *thug life* was what they wanted and this was a way that they could earn some street cred. Block once said during one of the PCO's many meetings that "with the whites, it ain't about money! Naw, it's all about appearances. How they look to their peers and the people around them. Being a drug dealer to white folks is all about them looking tough like they ain't the one to be fucked with. And we can offer them that. We can get our product into areas we normally wouldn't be able to and at lower cost, 'cause like I said, with whites, it ain't about the cash."

Moving into the other areas was easy once they started killing niggas on sight for trying to move weight or any kind of product. Small-time hustlers were lining up to be down with the PCO.

Everything was going according to plan. To keep things moving smoothly, the PCO started to make moves toward getting connections in City Hall and the PPD. This turned out to be easier than they had originally imagined. It seemed like every politician, cop, and city worker in general had their hand out looking for a piece of the pie. By this time, everyone knew what happed to Razmon, and they knew at whose hand he meet his gruesome demise. So from the street level, no one would even think of crossing Block and the PCO.

A couple of months later, and everyone from the streets on up shared that same sentiment. The PCO was not to be fucked with. Even back then, everyone thought that Block was the real head of the PCO, although in his mind, it was quite the contrary. Block meant everything that he said on the night the PCO was formed, that they worked together as one in all things, had loyalty to each other above all others. Every decision made had to be cleared by at least two of the three of them, but most were cleared by all three. Even though most of the planning came from Block, he never took any kind of credit for the success of the PCO, because in his mind, this was something that they had put together as one.

Unfortunately, not everyone saw it that way. This would prove to be a problem later on. It was also a problem that Block was aware of, but his biggest mistake was probably not doing anything about it.

Five months in, the PCO ran most of Philadelphia. They had their hands in almost everything, legit and nonlegit: drug stores, drug houses, car washes, drug fronts, etc., the list went on and on. Their influences were felt everywhere, from the crack house on the corner to the mayor's office, and anywhere in between. They had connections so high up in the police department that they were warned three days ahead of time when a raid or any type of major drug bust was going down so they could plan accordingly.

Life was good. D, Rock, and Block were pulling in money hand over fist, so much paper they couldn't spend it all, and at first, they definitely tried. They had the money, power, and the respect that they all wanted their whole lives, and they were living life to the full. Big houses, fast cars, fast bitches, mo' money, mo' alcohol—they definitely were living the good life. But they kept it all under control. They stayed focused and hungry. MOB became one of their main mission statements. Even without the drug money, their legit businesses were pulling in 40 percent of their revenue. Life was good.

But there was always that nagging feeling in the back of Block's mind that this had to end sometime. Although he never shared these thoughts with anyone—not even D—they were constantly there. This was one of the things that kept Block cautious and in check, because he knew that when you're on top, someone is always gonna be gunning for you. He also knew that particularly in black history, when one man has too much power or his group does too well, when they go down, the downfall came from within their own circle and rarely came from the outside. It was no secret that Block wasn't related by blood to Rock and D, and it also was no secret that Block and D were tighter than blood. But regardless, they all treated each other like family nonetheless.

But even from the beginning, it seemed that there had always been some sort of unspoken friction between Rock and K-Block. Maybe it was because Rock was always all about the streets—he did work in the streets, he did time for the streets, he had even been shot a couple of times because of the streets. K-Block, on the other hand, was as far as all that street shit was concerned— was a straight-up square. He held a regular job, lived in a regular home, had a regular wife and regular kids, and was just a regular dude.

While he was working for that pharmaceutical company, life was pretty good, and it was about that time that D came to live with him and his wife and kids, and Block always treated D like he was his very own brother. Block looked out for D in a way he wasn't used to. D was well on his way deep into the street life like his brother, Rock, but Kelly tried to steer him clear of that as much as he possibly could. D always respected Block for it and tried his best not to disappoint him. And even when he let the street shit get the better of him, Block never made him feel any type of way about it, and that was something D really appreciated. This could be why Block and Rock never truly saw eye to eye on everything, and when it looked as if they were ever gonna come to blows, D was always the one to smooth shit out between them. In a way, D was the glue that held the PCO together, because without him, Rock and K-Block could never coexist. But regardless of how they truly felt about one another, they were family. And on a normal day-to-day basis, they got along okay.

All the while that the PCO was climbing to the top of the Philadelphia drug game, K-Block often wondered how he got to this place in his life. After a lifetime of preaching from his father and pampering from his mother, surely it would seem to take more than a cheating wife to push him over the edge. Block allowed himself a moment to think. To think back to his childhood and remember.

He remembered he had a pretty good childhood—nothing worth complaining about, pretty average. His parents were good people, and they raised both their children up in the church. Sunday school every Sunday morning (no exceptions), Bible study at the church every Tuesday and Thursday nights. And on Wednesdays, after their homework was done, Bible study at home. Their parents weren't strict per se, but they didn't tolerate a lot of worldly influences in their home. That meant they couldn't watch a whole lot of TV, and the only radio station they were allowed to listen to were gospel. Despite that, Block remembers a really happy childhood.

It wasn't till he started getting interested in girls that it seemed his problems began. During his teenage years, he was out of control, running the streets, staying out past his curfew. He also had some near run-ins with the law, but was never caught, and even if they suspected it, his parents could never prove it.

That's where most psychologists start, isn't it? Block thought. *With the childhood.* Couldn't find an answer to his liking there. *Maybe the marines?*

Block continued his search for an answer to how he got like this, because he knew that it all changed along the way somewhere. He just could not pin down where. He had spent a couple of years in the marines after he got out of high school and before he got married.

Maybe! Yeah! Maybe that was where it all started for me.

Block had always wanted to be a marine growing up. He didn't know why. He was just drawn to it. But he wasn't your typical jarhead though. Block was very intelligent, and although, he could deal with the harshness of daily rigorous marine training, he had a hard time following orders. All the armed services had their own—although similar—ways to break new cadets and mold them to their way of life and thinking.

Block would not be broken, and when you're a new marine cadet with a chip on your shoulder, life is very hard for you, and very soon, you realize that all your drill instructors have that very same chip on their shoulders—and most of the time, bigger chips that yours. Needless to say, this caused a lot of friction and trouble for a young Kelly in the marines. On more than one occasion, one of Block's drills would drop their garrison hat and put rank aside and dare Block to hit 'em. Like all marines, especially the drill instructors, they felt that they couldn't be beaten by anyone other than maybe another marine, and cadets weren't considered full-fledged marines until graduation.

Each time a drill would dare Kelly, he would take him up on that dare. More times than not, Kelly would knock one out with one punch. Needless to say, he took his fair share of ass-whoopings too. But he never backed down, which is why regardless of his attitude, when it was time for him to be discharged, he got an honorable one, because even if his COs didn't like him, they all had to respect him.

After basic training, Block was deployed to Iraq. He remembered seeing a lot of action on the front lines. He remembered doing a lot of shooting, but he mostly remembered being shot at, and shot at a lot. But still, none of that bothered him. He knew that was just all part of his job. In fact, the more Block thought about it, the more he just concluded maybe this was just the way he was from the beginning and maybe it just never manifested itself till now. While he was at home with his parents, there was never a need, and when he was married, it was just always a part of him. He was just so practiced in holding back. Now that it was just him, he could finally let it all hang out.

Wow! Block thinks as he starts to laugh, *I really am crazy!*

Chapter 22

I'm Back, Niggas

Three weeks pass since Rock's disappearance, and there is still no word or sign of him anywhere. It is as if the earth just swallowed him up. Business is still booming, of course. The fiends aren't gonna stop fiendin' no matter what. And PCO is still all about getting that paper.

That doesn't mean that they still aren't looking for Rock though. D is stressing harder than ever, and Tracy is getting lockjaw trying to keep him calm. Tracy is working double time giving D head every day, sometimes three to four times a day, just to keep his mind off things.

For Block, it is pretty much business as usual. Although he wants Rock to return safe and sound so things would get back to normal, he has this sinking feeling in his gut that when and if Rock did return, things would never be the same again.

Two more days pass, and still no word. D is sure his brother is dead, but he doesn't know where or by who. One thing is for sure: if he ever finds out, there would be hell to pay. D thinks while driving to meet Block at the spot. *What the fuck could have happened? Who the fuck would fuckin' dare to come at one of us? It doesn't make no sense.* D picks up his cell and calls Block.

"Sup, my nigga?" Block answers the phone.

"Yo, nigga, I'm gonna be a little late for the meeting. I gotta check some shit out first," says D.

"Yo, whatever, nigga. Meeting don't start without you anyway. What's up?"

"I don't know, Block. Something just don't sit right with me about Rock's disappearance. I gotta go check some niggas out. I'll call you if I find out anything."

"Yo, my nigga, you need some backup or what?" asks Block. "Naw, nigga, I got this. Just hold it down till I get there."

They hang up. D then dials another number on his cell. "Yo, nigga, I need to see you right now! Yo, I don't give a fuck what you doing. Now, nigga. Right the fuck now. I'm gonna be pulling up at your crib in ten minutes." D hangs up the phone. *This shit is real shady. I know ain't no nigga in the PCO crossing us like this. This shit got pig written all over it. Yeah, this defiantly smell like pig shit to me.*

Back at the spot, Block makes a call of his own. "Yo, Low, come on in. D might have a lead on Rock. I need you hear in case shit kicks off and we gotta move."

It is almost noontime. The spot was pretty much empty—niggas are either trappin' or nappin', getting ready to trap. Guards and lookouts stay posted up at the spot—mostly niggas who used to run with Rock. Block gets up from the old wooden desk that is in the office that is his normal post and looks out the window onto the ghetto. Thinking and talking out loud to no one, Block says, "Shit really fucked up now!"

The reply and cocking of the hammer from behind him would have startled him if he didn't know it was coming for the last three weeks. "Nigga, you ain't never lied!" says the voice from behind him.

"Vanessa, Vanessa!" D shouts as he bangs on her door. *"Vanessa, get the fuck down here!"*

Vanessa Lopez is the one-time driver of Commissioner Herbert Jackson, personally selected by the commissioner to join the Task Force and unknown to anyone but D, Block, and Rock, a full-time member of the PCO. D had known Vanessa from the hood. They used to run with the same crowd. Back when they were both youngsters, D used to fuck Vanessa on the regular—she was bisexual back then. Freaky as a muthafucka. That's why D liked her. She gave him his first three-way with her and her big-tittied girlfriend. Now Vanessa is just a straight dyke. She doesn't fuck with no niggas, but if he wants to, D could always hit that ass.

"Nessa!" shouts D as she opens the door.

"Yes! Hold on! What is it, papi?"

She answers the door wearing nothing but a see-through robe. D could see them big titties, and his dick gets immediately hard. He almost loses focus for a second and immediately regains his senses as to why he came here. He pushes his way by her and into the house. "Tell whoever the bitch is you fuckin' to leave now!" He knows she must be in here eating some pussy, because Nessa never got all sexy when she was home unless she was fuckin', and all the burning candles she had lit around the house is a sure sign.

Nessa hurries to the bedroom and less than a minute later comes out escorting a fine, brown-skinned bitch half-dressed. She hurries her past D and out the door. D couldn't help but check out that ass as it goes by. He would have to set up another three-way with Nessa and that fine-ass bitch soon. But first, it's down to business.

"I'm only going to ask this shit once. If I don't get the answer I like"—D pulls out his gun—"I'll fuckin' kill you right here, right now."

"Papi, what are you talking about? What's wrong?" says Vanessa.

"It's been damn near a month since my brotha's been missing and nothing. Now I know for a fact ain't no nigga on the streets got the balls to go after one of us, so the only logical conclusion I can come to is that the fucking pigs have something to do with this shit. Now you're gonna tell me what I wanna know, and you're gonna tell me right now, or you ain't gonna see another birthday."

Nessa normally liked it when D talked all rough with her, but this time, it's different, and she knows she had better not fuck with him. So she starts spilling her guts, telling everything she knows about Rock's disappearance. She tells him how the day when Rock pulled up at City Hall to take out the commissioner, they were waiting for him; how they had been waiting for him ever since the press conference calling the PCO out. She told him how the commissioner and the mayor had this planned from the beginning, using themselves as bait, how there were sharpshooters all around City Hall in strategic locations, lying in wait. As soon as the windows on the BMW went down, everyone in the car was silently laid down with high-powered rifles with silencers with the exception of Rock, who was taken into custody without incident.

"We moved on him so quickly, no one around knew what, if anything, was going on. He was taken into custody and transported out of the scene swiftly by two officers. Another jumped right in the car he was driving and drove it to a remote location, all in the time span that it takes for a traffic light to turn from red to green," says Vanessa.

"So tell me again why the fuck you didn't call me," says D.

"D, you gotta understand, the commissioner is really on a fuckin' mission. Everyone in the unit who is single or with no family in the city to speak of was assigned twenty-four-seven duty to watch and interrogate your brother. That includes me. Everyone in the unit with a family got to go home once a week in sets of twos. This thing with apprehending your brother was given top priority, and the commissioner wasn't going to allow any type of breach of security or risk any leaks getting out and you guys finding out what happened to Rock. All communications were cut off. All cell phones were confiscated. E-mail and Internet access as well as access to the landlines were closely monitored. You have to believe me, I would have called you if I could. Some of us single people was getting a little stir-crazy, so the commissioner gave us a leave for a couple of hours, you know, to let off some steam. So you know how I do. I called up one of my bitches and was gettin' it in when you called. I was gonna call you as soon as I got done, I swear."

"So what I'm hearing is that your top priority was to get a fuckin' nut rather than call me and tell me about my brother?"

"No, D, really, it's not like that!" exclaims Nessa.

"You know it seems like it's exactly like that, bitch! You have fucking forgot who you're fucking talking to. You fucking forgot where your loyalties lie, bitch! And since you're so fucking forgetful, I'm gonna fucking forget to let you live." And with that, D unloads half a clip from his SIG right into Nessa's midsection. She screams as she hits the floor, then silence.

D walks over to her and kneels beside her and kisses her on the forehead. "Damn, bitch, I was really looking forward to fucking you and your girl. Oh well!"

As D starts to rise and get up to leave, Nessa with her last breath, grabs his hand and says, "We let him go."

"So here we are, huh, nigga?" says Block as he staggers from the window to the big wooden desk and takes a seat. The bullet hit him in the left shoulder and went straight through. Not enough damage to kill him, but it sure hurt like a muthafucka.

"Yeah, muthafucka. Here the fuck we are!" replies Rock.

"About fuckin' time. What took you so long, nigga? I always thought you was kinda slow," says Block.

"Muthafucka, don't even act like you saw this shit comin'! You see, that's why I could never really stand your punk ass always thinking you know shit. Acting all like you some big-ass gangsta-brain muthafucka an' shit. Nigga, you ain't no muthafuckin' gangsta. You a bitch-ass nigga. And today, nigga, you die," says Rock.

To Rock's surprise as he looks over the barrel of his gun, K-Block is laughing as he lights his cigar. "Muthafucka, you really are one big dumb, dense-ass nigga," Block replies as he continues to be unable to contain his laughter. "Muthafucka, Stevie Wonder could have saw this shit coming. You and I both know the only reason we were able to deal with each other this long was because of D. You are right about one thing: I ain't no muthafuckin' gangsta. I'm just a vicious-ass businessman. All of your so-called gangsters and Gs an' shit end up in one of three places: dead or in jail or in witness protection for snitchin'. Which one are you, G?" Block continues laughing.

"Muthafucka, what the fuck are you laughing at? Don't you know you're about to die?" says Rock, perplexed at the seemingly nonchalant Block. He was half-expecting him to beg for his life. But this reaction was the furthest thing from his mind.

"Nigga, what?" asks Block. "What? You expect me to start crying and shit, begging for my life? Nigga, please! Only one of us in this room is really afraid to die, and it ain't me, G!" Block continues to laugh.

"What the fuck are you laughing at?" shouts Rock, and he fires again, this time catching Block in the chest.

This one might kill him. It's bleeding real bad, but he's still alive and still laughing. "What the fuck are you waiting for, muthafucka? Kill me already. You big dumb muthafucka can't even get that done," Block says as he continues to laugh.

"The next one is going in your muthafuckin' dome. Let's see you laugh that off." Rock points his weapon, preparing to fire a third round.

Just then—

"*Rock!* What the fuck is going on? What the fuck are you doing?" shouts D as he enters the room. D looks over and sees Block sitting behind the desk, bleeding with two bullet holes in him.

"D, my nigga," says Rock, "you just in time to help me finish off this cocksucker."

"Finish off? What the fuck you talking about? What the fuck are you doing? I found out that the pigs grabbed you and was holding you all this time, but what the fuck is this shit you doing now?"

"I'll tell you what this is," says Block. "This is what happens when a regular, got-nothing, going-nowhere nigga gets some money and power. They don't know what to do with themselves. They already feel like the world owes them something. This is what happens when a regular, got-nothing, going-nowhere nigga starts to think he deserves more than his due. This, my brotha, is what happens when a G turns snitch. And I hate to be the one to break it to you, but this nigga right here that we call brother is that type nigga," says Block.

"*Shut the fuck up!*" yells Rock as he slaps Block with the barrel of his gun.

"*Yo, Rock!*" yells D. "What the fuck are you doing, man? This ain't how PCO roll, nigga. We family. What are you doing?"

"No, nigga," replies Rock, "*we* family. You and me. This nigga here ain't no fucking blood to us. And I think it's about time we made the PCO a true family business and cash this bitch-ass nigga out."

"Yo, Rock, what the fuck are you sayin'? We all been doing this thing for a minute. Rock, if it wasn't for K-Block steppin' up our game, we would have never crossed the fuck over to where we are. How could you even think to betray the trust we set this whole organization on? What the fuck are you thinking? What the fuck did those pigs do to you, nigga?" says D.

"*Yo, fuck this nigga!* We don't owe him shit. He didn't do nothing neither of us couldn't have done. And you talk about trust, nigga? You been wondering about your girl steppin' out on you lately? Well, who the fuck do you think she was stepping out with? This nigga that you trust so damn much. That night at the Pic, you said your girl wasn't home when you got there, right? And who was it that came strolling through all late an' shit. Yo, fuck this nigga. We don't need him, bro. We can do him right now, and all we have built will be ours. Split two ways is a helleva lot better than three.

"And to answer your question, what the pigs did was basically torture me for three fucking weeks. For the first two weeks, I basically told them to fuck off, but on the third week, I let them think that they broke me. Shit, I even let them put a wire on me and everything." Rock opens his shirt to reveal the device. "Stupid pigs don't know about all the high-tech, soundproofing, antibug, and antiwire shit we got installed all through this house. Right now they outside listening to static an' shit. They wanted me to come in here and get Block and you to spill your guts and shit. They said they couldn't go to court on just my word. Too much chance that y'all would beat the case and walk. Got my own plans though. I figured we waste this nigga and burn this place to the ground, sneak out the back during the confusion an' shit and set up shop in a new location, maybe Jersey. How's that sound, nigga?" Rock asks.

Now D's head is spinning. He can't believe what he is hearing. Betrayed by Block? And all the things Rock was saying, he couldn't believe it. D didn't even notice that he had drawn his gun, but he wasn't aiming at anyone yet. "Block, say this isn't true. You and Tracy, nigga—this can't be right."

"D, you know me better than anyone, and I think you know that I would die rather than betray you. With that being said, you now have a choice to make. If I'm lying, you and Rock have to finish me off right here and now, but if I'm not, you have to do Rock—a decision I never wanted you to have to make. That's why I took Rock's bullet that night. 'Cause when it comes down to it, I would never ask or expect you to kill your own blood. But as you can see, I'm in no condition to shoot anyone. Shit, if I don't get patched up soon, I'm as good as dead anyway. So this whole conversation is pointless."

"You damn right it's pointless, 'cause you gonna die, nigga. You don't expect my own flesh and blood to kill me, do you? Fuck you, nigga," says Rock, and he prepares to finish off Block.

"Don't pull that fuckin' trigger, Rock!" says D as he takes aim at Rock's head. "Don't you fuckin' do it!"

"Yo, D, what the fuck you doing, man? You gonna believe this nigga over me, your own brother?"

"Don't matter right now, Rock, what I believe. I ain't gonna let Block die, and I ain't gonna let you kill him either."

"Damn it, D. We don't have time for this bullshit. I told you the cops are right outside, and they only gonna stand by for so long. We gotta do this, nigga. Set the fire and get the fuck out," exclaims Rock.

"Can't let you do it, Rock," says D. "I'm gonna kill this muthafucka, D, and you just gonna have to shoot me to stop me."

"Don't do it, Rock, Don't fuckin' do it!" yells D. *"I'm not playin'. I will fuckin' shoot. Don't do it!"*

"He's dead, D, and I don't think you can shoot me to stop me." Rock then turns his head to finish the job.

Bang!

CHAPTER 23

Bang! You're dead

"Sir, we still cannot get a signal on Rock's wire. All we get is static."

"Keep at it, Officer. If we don't get a signal and he's not out in five minutes, were going in," says the commissioner. *I really hope he doesn't come out*, thinks Herb. *I would love to go in there and deal with these muthafuckas once and for all. 'Cause if we go in, ain't none of the PCO coming out alive.*

"What the fuck?" shouts D as he watches his brother hit the floor, dead with a hole in the side of his head.

Block looks up, bleeding and in an extreme amount of pain, as D turns around to find Low standing there, his gun still smoking and still pointed where Rock was standing.

"What the fuck are you doing, Low?" screams D as he points his gun at him.

"I did what had to be done. What you couldn't," says Low.

"Who the fuck do you think you are? You think you can just come in here and handle our business? I ought to fuckin' do you right now," D says, pointing his gun at Low.

Low lowers his gun and replies, "You gotta do what you gotta do. Just like I did what I had to. But before you take me out, you should know that it wasn't K-Block who was doing your girl behind your back. It was Rock."

"What the fuck you sayin'? How the fuck you know about any of this shit?" says D.

"I don't know how long he's been fuckin' your girl, but I do know he was fucking her pretty regular. And the two weeks you and Block was gone and left him in charge, he was at your crib hittin' that almost before you got on the road good. I also know that he started just saying 'Fuck it' to the orders Block left about the commissioner almost immediately, and that's what got his ass busted in the first place," replies Low.

"Then if you knew all this shit, why the fuck didn't you tell us before now?" D is now shaking with rage, gun still pointed at Low's head.

"Because I'm loyal to the PCO above all others. And until now, it wasn't my place to intercede. Feel me?"

"D, put your gun down. You know he's right," says Block.

D lowers his gun and turns to face Block. "Block, what the fuck are you saying? How can you say he was right? He just shot my brother, man!"

"D, he just shot *our* brother. Who, by the way, shot me first. D, you know our rules, our code, better than anybody. You knew that it would eventually come to this three weeks ago, when we found out what Rock had done," says Block.

"Fuck! Fuck, fuck!" shouts D.

"D, D!" shouts Block. "We gotta get the fuck outta here, man. If the cops have got Rock bugged, then it won't be too long before they come the fuck in here 'cause he ain't coming out. We gotta go, man, and sort all this out later. Low, give me a hand."

Low heads over to the desk and helps Block out of the chair. He puts Block's arm around his neck and heads for the door. Before anyone notices, D has put Block's other arm around his neck and is helping Low carry Block out.

As they come from around the desk and head for the door, D couldn't help but look down on the lifeless body of his brother one last time and silently wish him peace. As they head for the doorway, D speaks. "So what the fuck we gonna do now? If the cops have this place surrounded, how we gonna get out?"

"First, we gotta head for the cellar," says Block.

"The cellar? We'll be sitting ducks down there, Block."

"You gotta trust me, D."

So the three head down the stairs toward the normally guarded heavy metal door. All the guards had been put on alert when they left the office. They were all posted around the inside of the house, waiting for the cops, and as if on cue, as soon as they close the door behind them, here come the cops, guns blazin'. The guards were told to hold off the cops for as long as possible and to move out to the backyard, to the house on the left, as soon as they were given the signal.

Low, D, and Block reach the bottom of the steps. This was Block's private area. D had only been in here himself a handful of times, and Low had never been past the upstairs door except for once to clean up a body. They move to a small room in the back.

The room was very small, very sparse. The only things in it are a small wooden desk and chair in the middle of the floor. Block instructs Low to turn off the light in the room they just came from and close the door. Once the door is closed, Block instructs Low to pull the string hanging from the light two times and open the left desk drawer.

Low thinks Block has lost too much blood and is starting to get delirious, but he does as he is told, and a door behind the small desk pops open. Low pushes the door open further to reveal an escape tunnel that seems to go on for a couple of blocks. Low and D are beyond surprise at this.

"What the fuck is this, Block?" says D.

"It's plan B," says Block. "Let's go. Low, be sure to close the door behind us."

The three men enter the tunnel, and Low closes the door behind them. instantly, the drawer to the small desk closes. The light in the small room turns off, and the lights in the bigger room—the workshop where Block does his special work—turns on, and with that, a small inconspicuous timer under the workbench starts to count down.

"Commissioner, we have breached the perimeter. The guards are starting to retreat farther into the house. Our teams in the back report they are starting to notice extra movement in the rear. Still no sign of Rock or the other two."

"Okay, good. Let's move in."

"Sir, I think—"

"I know what you think, Sergeant. You think I should stay back at least until the house is secure, but not today. I'm gonna finish this firsthand and face-to-face with those bastards."

With that, Commissioner Jackson starts to move in with his team full force. They manage to make it to the third floor where the office is—the office where the PCO made life-altering and life-ending decisions—and he now sees why Rock never came out. Herb looks around as if he can hear the walls speak and tell their many stories of plans, plots, mayhem, and murder. Just then, Herb's thoughts are interrupted by a loud explosion on the rooftop then, seconds later, another explosion from the cellar.

"What the fuck was that?" says Herb. Just at that moment, Commissioner Herbert Jackson—twenty-year vet of law enforcement, protector of the people, an upstanding public servant—realizes too late . . . *"It's a trap!"* His warning goes unheard due to the third explosion that goes off right in that very room.

The three walk for a couple of blocks and hear the explosions behind them.

"What the fuck was that?" asks Low.

"All part of the plan. Keep going. We're almost there," replies Block.

They keep walking and end up in another basement. They go through this new basement to the attached garage. There waiting was a black Chevy Impala SS. Nothing too conspicuous. Not the normal 745s they are used to riding in.

D helps Block into the backseat and jumps in beside him, and Low jumps into the driver's seat. The keys are already in the ignition. Low starts the car, hits the garage door opener on the sun visor, and they are off.

"Head to the Northeast airport. I got a plane waiting," says Block. He then reaches in his pocket and pulls out his cell, hits the speed dial number 1. "It's time," says Block to the person on the other end, and he then hangs up.

Thirty minutes later, the three are on a plane headed for Cuba. There is a doctor waiting to take care of Block's wounds on the plane. When he is finished, D and Low come to check on him.

"Yo, Block, what the fuck is all this? What is going on?" asks D.

"Well, my brother," a now very drugged-up and tired K-Block replies, "this is plan B. You see, it's always wise to have a backup plan. Doesn't matter who you are. If history has taught us anything, it has taught us that eventually, all empires fall. It's just a matter of time. So it behooves us as leaders of an empire to expect and plan for these events to happen. I started planning for these events the night we formed the PCO. I set various things in motion without your or Rock's knowledge, because it had to be kept secret. The slightest leak could compromise everything.

"When Rock was taken, it would have been too easy for him to tell the police about the escape tunnel. Unfortunately, everyone who knew about the tunnel's existence had to be killed, which included a handful of greedy construction workers, engineers, and such. The pilot for this plane and the doctor who patched me up had no idea who was keeping them on retainer till we showed up here today. They just kept joyfully banking the $100,000 cash I sent them every two weeks. They don't know it yet, but they not gonna make it back to the States. On my trip to Cuba three weeks ago, not only did I get us a better rate on the product we sell, but I also made arrangements with my man Pablo for us to live, recover, and plan there quite comfortably for a little while. A little Cuban hideout right next to Castro's place, only about ten to twelve acres of land or so."

"So what you're saying is you couldn't trust me? You couldn't tell me any of this 'cause it would have been a breach of security? That's real fucked up, Block," says D.

"Naw, nigga, what I'm saying is this was something I had to do without you for you, nigga. Hopefully, you'll understand after a little time in Cuba. Now I'm a little tired. Wake me when we get there, niggas."

"Yo, Block, you said we're gonna live and plan there. Plan for what?" asks Low.

"Our comeback, nigga. What else?" replies Block.

Printed in the United States
By Bookmasters